What an inspired idea—to tell the story of a brilliant poet's life through a series of brilliant poems!

Hemphill's poetry radiates with passion, taking us on a harrowing journey deep into the heart of Plath's darkness. This beautiful book leaves us uplifted, knowing that despite the tragedy that befell her, Plath's words will live on after her to "do some good . . . save someone lost."

—Sonya Sones, author of *What My Mother Doesn't Know* and *Stop Pretending: What Happened When My Big Sister Went Crazy*

Your Own, Sylvia

A Verse Portrait of Sylvia Plath

by Stephanie Hemphill

Alfred A. Knopf New York

THIS IS A BORZOI BOOK PUBLISHED BY ALFRED A. KNOPF

Copyright © 2007 by Stephanie Hemphill
Jacket illustrations copyright © 2007 by John Ritter

www.randomhouse.com/teens

Educators and librarians, for a variety of teaching tools,
visit us at www.randomhouse.com/teachers

Library of Congress Cataloging-in-Publication Data
Hemphill, Stephanie.
Your own, Sylvia : a verse portrait of Sylvia Plath /
by Stephanie Hemphill. — 1st ed.
        p.   cm.
ISBN 978-0-375-83799-9 (trade)
ISBN 978-0-375-93799-6 (lib. bdg.)
1. Plath, Sylvia—Poetry.   I. Title.
PS3608.E49Y68 2007
811'.6—dc22   2006007253

Printed in the United States of America

March 2007

10   9   8   7   6   5   4   3   2

First Edition

for Cecile Goyette
and all those who love
or come to love Sylvia Plath

Acknowledgments

Thanks to Steve for having the vision to connect me to this project and for rekindling my love of Plath. Thanks to Adam for challenging me to expect more of myself and for his guidance with this book. Thanks to Jim for being my first reader and always my best advocate. Thanks to Jack Lienke, without whose help in acquiring photographs and digging up difficult details of research *Your Own, Sylvia* would be incomplete. I am also very grateful to Karen Kukil and the Smith Collection and to Professor Sylvia Vardell of Texas Women's University.

Your Own, Sylvia

Owning Sylvia Plath

A Reader
  Spring 2007

If the moon smiled, she would resemble you.
You leave the same impression
Of something beautiful, but annihilating.
  —from "The Rival" by Sylvia Plath

Who are you, Sylvia Plath?
A cold comet locked in place by gravity?
A glint in the cracked ceiling above my bed?

Something shimmers out of your chasm.
Your language feels like words
trapped under my tongue
that I can't quite spit out on my own.

Readers tremble over your pages,
believe you spell out
letter by letter
the words of their hearts.

What's your secret, Sylvia?
Are you the moon?
Or have you become bigger than that?
Are you the sun?

And I wonder,
who can possess the stuff of the sky?
  Can I?

Sylvia Plath signed many letters she wrote to her mother "Your own, Sivvy."

"The Rival" appears in Plath's famous poetry collection, *Ariel.*

Dearest, Darling, First Born

Aurelia Plath, Sylvia's mother
October 27, 1932

Child of sea and sand,
your face is mine
but you will be tall
with the dark eyes of your father.

When you cry
I will rock you and rhyme you,
feed you milk of my breast,
give you my diligence, my contract of love.

Big beautiful Sivvy,
we are alone in this hospital.
Grow accustomed
to the antiseptic white.

My baby, my duty,
I will rear you right.
Give you everything, buttons off my shirt.
You will be what I cannot.

Sylvia Plath was born in Boston on October 27, 1932, the first child of Otto Emil Plath, a professor of German and biology at Boston University (age forty-six), and Aurelia Schober Plath (age twenty-five). Sylvia's lifelong family nickname was Sivvy.

Aurelia Schober Plath graduated valedictorian of the 1928 class of Boston University, College of Practical Arts and Letters. Aurelia wanted to be a writer but could not face her father's disapproval.

Beekeeper, Penny-Pincher, Professor, Master of the House

Otto Plath, Sylvia's father
Circa 1936

If I do things best
why invite others in
to clutter my desk?
Why waste my nights
of valuable book study
with idle dinner prattle
or tucking the children into bed?

My daughter understands this
better than my wife—
fills her brain
with insect species, bits of verse,
beach sand. She dances well
and I applaud, then shoo her
upstairs to her mother's care.

I expect Sylvia to grow tall,
fill her palms with the mud
and mystery of the world—
fireflies and sparrows
darting across her sky.
I will observe her, set her right,
but never coddle her.

My old arms
have the strength to carry
papers, not children.
I am the long-reigning queen bee,
Aurelia, Sylvia, and Warren,
my workers, buzz as I dictate,
store my honey, keep the comb clean.

When I perish,
a new queen
will lead this little hive,
but until then
the house, wife, and children
conform to the direction
of my wings.

Warren Plath, Sylvia's brother, was born on April 27, 1935; in 1936 he would have been one year old.

Edward Butscher, in his book *Sylvia Plath: Method and Madness*, asserts, "For Sylvia Plath, even as the most casual reading of her poetry demonstrates, the central obsession from the beginning to the end of her life was her father, Otto Emil Plath. His life and, more importantly, his death, nine days after [Sylvia's] eighth birthday, left an imprint upon her imagination that time did not soften."

Sylvia's journals often compare and contrast Ted Hughes, her husband, with her father. Her famous poem "Daddy" is a good example of this.

The Day She Learned to Swim

Marian Freeman, a neighbor, Aurelia's friend
Spring 1937

Sylvia's little footprints
crisscross the sand
like lines to a treasure map.
She leads David, Ruth, and Warren
hunting crabs and shells, filling
pails with green sea glass.
She's so much a part of the ocean,
Sylvia's skin tans brown as the beach sand,
her curled, fourteen-karat hair
blazes like the noon sky.

Four years old and clearly
the sun in her mother's eye,
giving light to the moon rock
Aurelia has become.
I love them both, ache like Sylvia
is my own when she wades beyond
the sand bar and slips
under the water's edge,
her hands flailing, frantic
above the surface.

Aurelia and I tear off
the beach blanket,
knees deep in the tides
when Sylvia bobs forward,
her arms paddling
like fins, her head
triumphant above water—
already a mermaiden,
a sea nymph
cresting the wave.

The Plaths lived in Winthrop, Massachusetts, at 92 Johnson Avenue at this time.

Hurricane

Aurelia Plath
September 21, 1938

I sing to Sivvy and Warren,
hide them under my breast
while winds roar and water
seeps into the house.
Telephone poles snap.

I whisper fairy stories,
light verse into their ears
so that the memory of this
night will be melodic,
not nature's tantrum.

Sylvia clenches my hand.
She breathes my stories in,
her lips open like she's ready
to speak her own.

In September 1938 a major hurricane ripped through the Boston area. Winthrop,
the city's easternmost suburb, was hit the hardest. Sylvia writes about this storm in
her poem "The Disquieting Muses."

Point Shirley

Grammy Schober, Sylvia's maternal grandmother
1939

The Atlantic licks our back porch.
Its frothy foam salts my tomato
and rhubarb plants.

Across the street Boston Harbor stills,
purrs quiet as a sleeping cat
until the wind stirs it.

Grampy mortared a seawall
around our modest summer castle,
held back last year's hurricane.

Sivvy, my little grandbaby,
collects broken starfish in my jam jars,
feeds the creatures until they sprout new legs,

then chucks them back to sea.
I tell her we must pack up,
the renters arrive tomorrow.

I fib that the beach down the road
is just as nice as Point Shirley.
"But, Grammy, I feel safe here," she says.

I remove her hand from the ocean,
brush off her sandy feet,
and set floral stationery in front of her.

I point at the paper, tell her to write her mother a letter.
She must learn to love indoor activities too.
Sylvia picks up her pen.

Sylvia's grandparents still lived in the house Sylvia's mother, Aurelia, grew up in, 892 Shirley Street, a beach house on the southeasternmost tip of the peninsula Point Shirley in Massachusetts. They rented out the house in the summer and then permanently sold the house shortly after Sylvia's father died.

Losing a Limb

Specialist Dr. Harvey Loder
1940

Otto's leg vermilion,
toe enlarged and unhealed
after a simple bump,
Mrs. Plath looked shocked
at my diagnosis—
diabetes.

Could have been prevented,
all this suffering,
had the professor
ever
seen me.

I hate to tell a woman
she will likely be a widow at thirty-three.
Aurelia stares at me
with determined, red eyes,
too proud to cry.

For such a brilliant man
Otto was stupid about his health.
An expert in biology,
with a family history of diabetes
and an addict's sweet tooth,

Mr. Plath
should have read the signs.
I guess stubbornness
is also a dominant trait.
Those poor little kids.

Aurelia straightens her hat,
slips on gloves, leaves
my office with a polite,
tight-lipped "Thank you, Doctor,"
a ghost of the wife who entered.

Otto had never gone to a doctor until 1940, when he stubbed his toe and it turned
purplish-black. He was diagnosed with diabetes mellitus. Otto had been suffering
from diabetes symptoms for ten years, and by the time his illness was diagnosed it
was life-threatening. Gangrene set in and his leg was amputated in October 1940.
In the end bronchopneumonia and an embolism killed him. Treatment for diabetes in 1940 consisted of dietary restrictions and insulin shots—both of which
Otto rigorously applied, but too late to undo the damage.

Mother's Strength

Aurelia Plath
       1940

A legless father
hobbled into bed is one thing.
My dears will not see
their father coffined, lowered
into the stiff November ground.

Marian holds their hands.
I wave to Sivvy and Warren,
suck in my tears until the hearse
door closes. What will we do?
How will we survive?

These questions stream
down my face. I can't pat them away
with his monogrammed hankie.

Sivvy raged,
"I'm never talking to God again,"
when I told her
that her daddy had died.

She's fatherless and faithless—
I must remain solid for her,
provide her the tools
she needs to believe.

Otto Plath died in the hospital at 9:35 p.m. on November 5, 1940. Sylvia was eight and Warren was five and a half. Prior to her marriage, Aurelia had worked in a public library and for an insurance company, and had taught English and German at Brookline High School. When they married on January 4, 1932, Otto insisted that Aurelia quit working and become a full-time housewife and mother.

First Publication

Editor of the Boston Herald
1941

"Hey, Mickey, this 'Poem'
from an eight-year-old girl's pretty good,
starts out, 'Hear the crickets chirping,'
and she chirps she has plenty more
where this one came from."

Mickey scratches his bald spot,
"Nothing but stalled cars
and weather this edition.
What the heck, print her little poem."

Joe nods,
"What's the byline, Mickey?"

"Says her name's Sylvia Plath,
thinks she's gonna be a star."

"Poem," a sweet rhyming verse about crickets and fireflies, appeared in the Sunday *Boston Herald* on August 11, 1941, on the "Good Sport Page" of the children's section.

Maître d'Hôtel

Grampy Schober, Sylvia's maternal grandfather
Summer 1942

I keep my hands in my jacket pockets,
poke a finger through the hole
Grammy will stitch.

No coins, no peppermint sticks
for my grandbabies. I magnify
the paper, search for work that doesn't exist.

But as the boys and bombs fall overseas, I polish
my shoes. Newly hired to be maître d'hôtel,
I live my weeks away
from my family, board
with the fancies and the frivolous
at the Brookline Country Club.

At least the Christmas tree
will bear boxes and chocolates this year.
The little ones' patched stockings full of loot.

I hold my tongue at work.
German accents are
like leper scars. I nod my head.

I am good at taking care of others.
Still, I hoped at this age someone
would take care of me,

that I would lounge seaside,
my feet cool on the sand, not crammed
for ten-hour shifts in pinching shoes.

For thirty years Frank Schober, Sylvia's "Grampy," worked as an accountant at Dorothy Muriel Company. He lost his job just after Christmas in 1940, only a couple of months after Otto's death. Because money was tight for everyone, in early 1941 Aurelia asked her parents and brother to move into her home to help share expenses. Grampy was hired in the summer of 1942 to work at the Brookline Country Club, which was located in a wealthy Boston suburb.

Outpatient

Aunt Dorothy, Sylvia's maternal aunt
February 1943

My sister recovers
in my guest room
from a life that ulcerates her.
She swells acidic carrying
two children, a checkbook,
and a household on her shoulders.

Our parents help, but age
weighs them down.
Sylvia treads words to keep afloat,
all those library books, journals,
daily letters penned to her mother.

Sylvia writes more in a day
than I do in a month. My sister,
hand cradling her gut, pencil shaky
from sedation, scrawls on her stationery,
tries to keep pace with her daughter.

When Sylvia was ten, Aurelia suffered an acute gastric hemorrhage.

Aurelia kept Sylvia's letters in packets. She always intended to give them back to her someday.

Selfish

Warren Plath, Sylvia's brother
1942–1943

Mommy gave Sylvia
a blue cloth book
without words
where Sylvia puts words
each day.

I ask her what stories
are in there,
but Sivvy shakes her head,
locks the book under her bed,
says that the words are *hers,*
that the stories are *her* thoughts,
that the book is called a journal.

I tell Sivvy that I want one too.
I have lots to say.
She says, "No, you don't.
You're too little to say anything
important."

Mean, mean, mean,
I think under my breath.

When Warren was born, Sylvia said, "I wanted an Evelyn, not a Warren." According-
ing to Aurelia in her introduction to *Letters Home: Correspondence 1950–1963,*
"Between Sylvia and Warren there were often arguments just for the sake of discussion." Sylvia teased her brother and yet they were very close. Warren appreci-
ated Sylvia's writing and artwork, and this led to an enduring friendship. Both
children were excellent students, highly praised and highly competitive. Both left
their marks.

Best Friend

Betsy Powley, Sylvia's best friend in grade school
1943

Camps, fern huts, Girl Scout cookies,
suntans on my driveway,
Sylvia and I never stop. We travel
the globe in our backyard.

She books away to foreign lands,
ancient times, and I
trot beside her—
Tonto to her Lone Ranger.

I whisper that I have a crush
on Donnie Russell, and the next week
Sylvia passes me a note from him
asking me to the Sock Hop.

She wizards her way
through woods and fences,
makes things happen.
Sylvia sees a door
where other people see a wall,
but where will it lead?

Sylvia first attended Annie F. Warren Grammar School in Winthrop, but her mother held her back a grade from sixth grade to fifth when they moved to Wellesley. Otherwise, Sylvia would have been two years younger than her classmates. In 1943 she attended Marshall Livingston Perrin School. Betsy was her neighborhood friend in Wellesley.

Boy Crazy

Ruth Freeman, one of Sylvia's best childhood friends
1945, eighth grade

Between reading her novels
Sylvia dreams boys, drifts
down a river of crushes.
Each week she paddles
somewhere new.

First Perry Norton,
then Dick Mills,
followed briefly
by Dick Cunningham,
and now Wayne Sterling.

Betsy and I stagger to keep up
with her whirlwind of romance.
I'm simple, a one-crush-
at-a-time kinda girl,
but Sylvia's always more complex.

She juggles a few boyfriends,
then fixates on Philip McCurdy.
I beg her to write these loony boy-capades
down. She smiles crooked and says,
"Don't worry, Ruth,
these boys are fodder for my pen."

At thirteen, Sylvia developed a keen interest in boys. Her adolescent fascination was divided between boys and writing. Always ahead of her class in academics and behind them in years, she didn't seem to fear or look forward to puberty. In her junior-high years, she often felt awkward.

Why She Writes

Imagining Sylvia Plath
    In the style of "Never Try to Trick Me with a Kiss"
    1946

There's nothing she can't do or think or say.
Inside a book, she captures all that's lost.
She journals so her words won't fly away.

She chases boys for nothing more than play.
She sailors them, she ties them up in knots.
There's nothing she won't do or think or say.

She's fearless like a man, she gets all A's.
She smiles like a girl. Her lips are glossed.
She journals so her mind won't fly away.

It's hard, this life that holds her gifts at bay.
A good girl, she feels trapped and even crossed.
There's so much she can't do or think or say.

Her mother she vows never to betray.
She knows just what her clothes and schooling cost.
She journals so her anger floats away.

She dreams of Daddy shooing her astray.
She dances, studies, paints until exhaust.
So many things to do and think and say.
She journals so her words will fly one day.

Sylvia's "Never Try to Trick Me with a Kiss" was published in her school literary magazine, the *Phillipian*, when she was thirteen. The poem, a rejection of the belief that love and happiness can be permanent, appears in her Pulitzer Prize–winning *The Collected Poems*.

Plath returned to this poem's form, called a villanelle, often in her early writings, most famously in "Mad Girl's Love Song."

Crocketteer

Wilbury Crockett, Sylvia's high school English teacher
1947

Sylvia possesses
a "natural lyrical gift."

She radiates, uranium strong,
when exposed to philosophy, literature.

Rarefied as a Rembrandt,
a student like this appears once

in a teacher's career.
After years of chalkboards

and textbooks, I can siphon
the butterfly from the moths.

Sylvia's wings are luminous
and large, her name will be known.

Multi-faceted—
a co-editor of the school paper,

a guard on the basketball court,
she bows viola, earns ribbons

for her watercolors, pledges into
the sorority social scene.

Her masks diverse, I aim
to nudge Sylvia toward her genius.

Most of the population cannot
craft a proper sentence.

Sylvia Plath sculpts poems
out of air.

Wilbury Crockett taught English like a college seminar. The thirty students chosen to be part of his class remained with him as their English teacher for all three of their years in high school. Sylvia called Crockett "the teacher of a lifetime." They corresponded with each other throughout her life. We know from letters they exchanged that Crockett expressed concerns about Sylvia when she attempted suicide and when she married Ted Hughes. Many of the letters to and from Mr. Crockett are housed in the Lilly Library at Indiana University.

Mr. Crockett, according to Paul Alexander's biography of Plath, *Rough Magic*, told his class in October 1947 after reading some of Sylvia's poems aloud that she possessed a "natural, lyrical gift."

Demolition

Bruce Elwell, a boy Sylvia dated in high school
Summer 1949

I feed her bourbon
and ginger ale,
lounge her on the terrace,
so Sylvia feasts on
the black star-crowded sky.

It's not hard to make her lie down—
her back bends easily.
Dizzy in summer's heat,
Sylvia speeds, almost flames,
but then pushes hard on the brake.

At the stock car races
she wishes for a crash—
tango of metal and spark,
burnt tire fumes choking
her throat.

And as if on cue,
a car leaps into the stands.
Seven people mangled,
whirled away by ambulance swirl.
How Sylvia ignites after that.

Wildfire in the backseat,
we throttle, approach the finish line,
but she yanks the keys
from the ignition, hurls
them out the window.

Sylvia shrugs, an "I'm sorry"
tease in her eye,
she fastens the good-girl girdle
beneath her skirt.
I'll never ask her out again.

Sylvia struggled with issues of sexuality—how far should she go? It was imperative
to her that she remain labeled a "good girl," yet she desired to be sexually active.
Sylvia was outraged by the prevailing gender-biased double standards of sexuality
common in her day.

A Room of Her Own

Warren Plath
       1949

As I wave goodbye,
scholarshipped to Exeter,
Sylvia peers from behind
the blue gingham curtain
of the bedroom that used to be mine.

After years of bunking
with Mother, Sylvia has a bed,
a desk, and a door all her own.
I wonder, as I drive away,
if she's really sad to see me go.

Sylvia and Warren were two and a half years apart. Warren attended Phillips
Exeter Academy from 1949 to 1953 on a four-year scholarship. Exeter is a prep
school that grooms students for entrance into the Ivy League.

Heartbreaker

John Hall, a college boy Sylvia dated in high school
Fall 1949, Sylvia's senior year

Without a wet eye of remorse,
Sylvia tells me that she's dating
two other boys, does not want to see me
anymore, after I fast-pedaled myself
from Williams straight to her door.

I replicate that smile of hers—
those painted lips without a twitch
or tic, without breath—
on my kisser,
but I am a terrible phony.

My watery eyes betray me,
shrink me into infancy.
I stagger to my car, hating her
as I slouch over the steering column
and my head shakes with sobs.

Another sad sack
in Syl's string of flings.
I thought I was special.
I don't really hate her,
but I boil at the way she's reduced me.

Taller and older than she is,
still, Sylvia pats me on the head
like I'm her kid brother.
"There, there, little Johnny," she croons
as she pushes me out the door.

In her junior year of high school alone, Sylvia dated about twenty boys. It was customary to date boys who were a few years or grades older. She dated college boys she met through friends of friends and family introductions. Sylvia also lived in a college town, Wellesley, although most of the boys she dated attended other colleges, such as Williams College and Denison University. Many of Sylvia's dating escapades are chronicled in her diaries and journals.

Valedictorian

Bradford Principal Samuel Graves
June 7, 1950

Sylvia finishes first
in her class, to no one's
raised eyebrows.

A freight train
furying down the tracks,
I hope in college she'll find
some "fun," not just
gold stars and blue ribbons.

She demands perfection
from herself,
the curl of her hair precise,
her argument against nuclear
disarmament exact.

Her shoulders rarely at ease—
it exhausts me to watch her.

I wonder why we create skyscraper
expectations in our youths today?
Do we fear it's too late to build our own?

Sylvia was seventeen when she graduated from high school in 1950. There were 158 students in her class. She knew at the time she was going to attend Smith and had won a couple of scholarships, one for $850 from Smith Student Aid and one from Wellesley's Smith Club for $450. These scholarships made it possible for Aurelia to afford to send Sylvia to Smith.

Smith was founded in 1871 to be a school for women that was academically equal to colleges for men. By 1950 Smith had become one of the premier undergraduate institutions in the country. Smith enrolled only 2,400 students, 600 per class, when Sylvia attended.

Lookout Farm

Cyrus Jeness, farm foreman at Sylvia's summer job
Summer 1950

Summer's frying-pan hot.
That beanpole blond girl
all the farmhands eyeball and drool over
wipes her brow backhanded.

She's stronger than you'd think,
pulls eight-hour days
same as the boys,
harvests beans and radishes

like a plow horse,
but then mans the roadside stand
like a shop lady,
handling customers with kidskin gloves.

That Sylvia's not all bronzed
angel, she does her share of devilin',
walks rickety barn planks
up to that German boy's loft.

We catch her red-faced,
bruise-lipped, sheepish,
as she slinks down
among the hay bales.

I'm sure not much happened,
but Sylvia's face froze, blushed guilty,
like she was caught—
hand in the owner's purse.

Sylvia wrote about this episode in her journals. She started her job as a field hand on June 10, 1950. Lookout Farm was located in Natick, Massachusetts.

Paper Doll

Eddie Cohen, University of Chicago student
Summer 1950

I read her first story in national
circulation in my sister's *Seventeen*
magazine. The tiny photograph
reveals the author's blond curls
and slightly askew smile.

I had to write her, see if
the glimmer of more, of something
real and dangerous I feel beneath
her words, bears out.
She pen-pals me back.

Infatuated with her cursive,
I flip over this cutout cutie,
this girl about to enter Smith
to whom I fashion my letters.
She could be my paper doll
come to life.

Eddie Cohen read Sylvia's story "And Summer Will Not Come Again" in the
August 1950 edition of *Seventeen* magazine. Eddie and Sylvia wrote each other
letters. They did not meet in person until March 1951, when Eddie drove out to
Smith as a surprise to meet her.

Dropout

Ann Davidow, Sylvia's roommate
first semester freshman year in Haven House
Fall 1950

Smith drains. I am not
like these girls.
I have met only one girl
who understands.

Sylvia Plath doesn't fit into the Smith uniform
or country-club chic, doesn't wear
the blue-blooded pearls either. While Sylvia
overcompensates for this,

I slump into the cafeteria,
oversleep for class.
I can't catch a wave in this place,
can't even wade into the Smith waters.

Sylvia dives into her studies,
reads ahead of the semester schedule
like someone's shooting
a gun at her heels.

She types her papers
a week before the due date
while I linger at the shoreline,
bury my toes in the sand.

The tides here are too rough.
I sink here, happy only when I hoard
my little blue sleeping pills,
stash the blades of my razor.

I accumulate a drawer
of drop-out devices,
so by December I can escape
to a Merry Christmas.

I wish I could be
more like Sylvia.

She calls me into her waves,
says she'll buoy me.
But I depart in the new year,
never to return to Smith.

Ann Davidow remained a close friend and correspondent of Sylvia's until Sylvia's death.

Money Well Spent

Olive Higgins Prouty, Sylvia's benefactor
Winter 1950

What pleasure to know
that my scholarship goes
to such a talented delight—
Sylvia Plath. I write and invite

her to my Brookline expanse,
the mansion financed
by bestsellers and radio play.
I intend to guide this protégée

into stories about her real life—
romance, desire, and family strife,
not make-believe thrillers with knives,
but tales of homemakers, trapped little wives.

I will mother Sylvia, foster her
and support her work. Posture for her
a woman writer's way.
In the hopes that someday

she'll find great renown.
Her words will resound,
ethereal, soaring,
and unbound.

Olive Higgins Prouty was the sponsor of Sylvia's scholarship at Smith. She remained a steadfast mentor and devoted friend to Sylvia. Mrs. Prouty was best known for her novel *Now, Voyager*, which was made into a Bette Davis movie, and for *Stella Dallas*, a novel that was adapted into both a Barbara Stanwyck movie and a popular radio serial.

Inconsiderate

Eddie Cohen, University of Chicago student
March–April 1951

Dear Rude One,
who do you think you are?
I drove sleep-deprived
a day across country
to visit you and you played
stranger to me, awkward
after months of letters.
Disappointed with
my unshaven face,
you treated me like
a fledgling C student
unfit to commingle
among the A class.

Now you mute me out,
don't respond to my angry
letters. I guess you're just
another Smithie snob, the blond
gone all the way to your head.
Do you lie in all your letters
or just the ones you postmark to me?
I may have let you down
with my Christmas stocking
of apples and oranges,
but you have crushed me,
given me a sock of coal
when I expected a gold medal.

Eddie visited Sylvia of his own volition. She did not ask or encourage him to come. Their meeting was awkward, and it is chronicled in letters and in Sylvia's journal.

New Roommate, New Friend

Marcia Brown, Sylvia's second Smith roommate
and lifelong friend
Winter–spring 1951

Sylvia Plath, the writer
of bulletin-board fame,
ascends the stairs
to move in with me.

We fit like Lincoln Logs,
notch together at pleasant angles,
both of us scholarships, working hard
to maintain the high Smith standards.

My mother adores Sylvia,
lets me travel to Manhattan,
the lair of corruption,
with her.

No one knows that Sylvia
straightens her sock drawer
four times a day, her sleep light
and infrequent as an infant.

She writes more in a day
than most people compose
in a month. Her eccentricities,
even her nose-picking, enchant me.

And I ground her.
She is a blue balloon
tethered to my wrist
pulling me in the wind.

I line up babysitting jobs
for us. I want to keep us close
both summer and school year.
She is my chosen sister.

I love Sylvia like an earlobe,
like she's a delicate, necessary
part of me. Sometimes I think
we form a goddess of two brains
and one body. I hope we stay
Siamese close forever.

Marcia and Sylvia knew each other from 1951 until Sylvia's death. Sylvia was a
bridesmaid in Marcia's wedding and always counted her as one of her best friends.

Summer 1951

Imagining Sylvia Plath
        In the style of "Two Lovers and
        a Beachcomber by the Real Sea"

She is bathing beauty. Sea-spun again.
    The waves kiss her ankles.
A day off from tending the children,
    She writes, she suns, she gathers her cockles.

In the ocean foam she sprouts fins, washes her face.
    Her anxious tides disintegrate under water.
If only she could hold summer's smooth embrace
    All year, maybe warmth would envelop her.

She combs her locks, combs the beach
    For shells like a child.
She stills by the waves, her language at peace.
    Yesterday's work expired.

Luxuriant fruit de la mer, gold glimmers of light.
    The day folds like a sheet.
Tomorrow will be work. She and Marcia dance into night,
    No boys to flaunt or tempt.

Can she not be happy alone on the sand
    With her letters and stories?
Why must she conform, attach to a man?
    She shivers in the dark breeze.

They call her into their water, the voices and the waves.
But she can't wade out to the bar yet.
She can't comprehend speaking a language that brave.
She turns housebound. For now, she retreats.

Over the summer of 1951 Sylvia worked as a mother's helper in Swampscott, Massachusetts, for Dr. and Mrs. Frederick Mayo and their three children. Marcia Brown was a mother's helper for another family down the street. The poem "Two Lovers and a Beachcomber by the Real Sea" deals with the conflict involving mind, belief, and imagination—common themes in Plath's poetry as she struggles to use her art for her own personal salvation. "Two Lovers . . ." was awarded the Glascock Prize during Sylvia's senior year at Smith. The poem can be found in her *The Collected Poems* as part of the "Juvenilia" section.

Patriarchy

*Dick Norton, Sylvia's on-and-off boyfriend throughout college
1951–1952, Sylvia's sophomore year*

If only Sylvia
would give up

her silly notions
of being a woman

of letters, and cultivate
her culinary skills,

social graces,
maternal instincts,

and all manners
becoming a doctor's wife.

Harvard Med behind me,
I will provide all that we need.

Sylvia is lovely,
but uppity.

Raised in the same town,
she should be my perfect

match. I can make her
so—adjust her skirt

to the right length,
teach her to darn

my socks correctly.
We are destined to be

a magazine couple.
If only she behaves

as I, the dominant gender,
demand. As I see fit.

Sylvia dated Dick starting in the winter of 1951, though to his dismay not exclusively until the winter/spring of 1953. Dick wanted to marry Sylvia, but Sylvia felt she and Dick were too similar to be right for each other as husband and wife. Dick pressed Aurelia in March 1953 as to why Sylvia would not marry him, and that pretty much marked the beginning of the decline and end of their romance.

Incurable Romantic, and Yet

*Marcia Brown, Sylvia's second Smith roommate
and lifelong friend
1951–1952*

She said the night was March and black
and that the hill where he kissed her
and enveloped her in his arms
was a sea of grass and she rooted
to the ground like a sapling,
like it was natural and yet
all created for her moment of romance.

Sylvia brooms through boys,
always hopeful that
one will catch her, will catch
her eye for more than a moment,
for more than a few journal entries.
She gets swept up, wants to be caught,
but by a worthy suitor, a man
of more than muscles and brains.
A man who shimmers, who is knightly,
not a man-as-mirror in which Sylvia
views only herself. She keeps trying
them on, brings her boys to the tailor
with hope and lust in her eye.
But even with straightened seams
and new lapels, no man
quite fits her, yet.

Sylvia records the feelings expressed in the above poem in her journal, entry fifty-eight, in *The Unabridged Journals of Sylvia Plath*.

Patient

Nurse at the Smith infirmary
*   1951–1952, Sylvia's sophomore year*

Poor girl suffers
from sinusitis,
only relief she gets
is when she's laid up here,
snuffing her cocaine nasal spray.
Flattened as a tire,
that Sylvia works herself
to the brink until she is
raw nerve, until she collapses.

My mama always said
maladies are the body's way
of asking for a slower pace.
But there is a blue violence
about this patient.
She has checked herself
in here three times now.
Guess it's better than checking
herself out. I hope we cure
what ails her.

Sylvia's sinusitis was an acute problem since early childhood. The doctors took her bouts seriously. At this time Sylvia was treated only for a physical illness. She was not referred to a therapist or psychiatrist.

Summer Job 1952

Mr. Driscoll, Sylvia's supervisor at The Belmont

A problem case,
that's what she is.

Not a talented waitress.
I assign her to the side room
to serve our staff, not our guests.

She snubs her nose,
makes plea and fuss
that she needs tips
to make this gig worthwhile.

I listen, shake my head,
tell her she lacks qualifications,
lacks skills.

She huffs
out of my office
like a boiling teapot,

then proceeds to gallivant
until dawn every night,
always on the arm
of a different boy.

Proves me right.
Still, I pity her.

I've needed cash
a day or two in my life.

So I throw this pup
a bone, offer Sylvia
an extra thirty dollars a week
to change the bed linens.

Turns me down cold
as an icebox. Ungrateful,
these youngsters. Lazy.

Maybe she thought she'd flirt
her way into an apron
of dollars, shine the guests
her silver-dollar smile.
I offer work for compensation.

Guess she won some
girl's magazine contest,
wrote a story.

Now I hear she's sick,
sent home to recuperate.

Phone call says she's not returning.
Can't say I'm sorry to see her go.

The Belmont was a resort hotel in West Harwich-by-the-Sea, Massachusetts.
Sylvia wrote about this waitressing job in her journals.

Prophecy

Harold Strauss, Editor in chief,
Alfred A. Knopf
Summer 1952

I chuck the *Mademoiselle* magazine
snatched from my daughter's bureau
on the acquisition meeting table.

"I want all of you to read this
prizewinning story, 'Sunday at the Mintons','
by Sylvia Plath." My secretary distributes

carbons to the staff. I inhale half
my cup of joe. Black, steamy, it burns
the roof off my palate.

"Mark my words,
this girl will publish with us
someday."

In June 1952, Sylvia received a telegram saying that she had won one of the two *Mademoiselle* College Fiction Contest first prizes and would be awarded $500. "Sunday at the Mintons' " can be found in Plath's collection of essays and short stories, *Johnny Panic and the Bible of Dreams*. Knopf did publish Sylvia's first collection of poetry, *The Colossus and Other Poems*, in the United States on May 14, 1962, after many delays.

Job Number Two

Margaret Cantor, wife in the family Sylvia nannied
Summer 1952

My husband hands Sylvia
the oversize check our children
constructed on manila art paper
and that he signed over to Miss Plath.

A million dollars for the million ways
we are grateful to have had Sylvia
help with our children this summer.

A magnolia, she brought beauty
and fragrance to our home,
enriched our little ones, was a radiant
influence of decorum and hard work
for my teenage daughter.

I tell Sylvia I would recommend her
for any job, to please let me know
if I can ever be of help to her. I love Sylvia
like a daughter, like a sister, like family.

I wish the summer would never end.
Sylvia smiles, dishes me a piece
of her chocolate layer cake, so devil rich
it must be a sin, and says, "Me too."

The Cantors vacationed in Chatham, Massachusetts. They had advertised for a mother's helper in the *Christian Science Monitor*. Sylvia worked for them for six weeks. She was included as part of the family. In her journals she writes, ". . . Life: full, rich, long, part of the family, growing to know them and their quietnesses, their laughters, their convictions, and always subtly probing, questioning, the core—Christian Science."—July 25, 1952.

Proud

Olive Higgins Prouty, Sylvia's benefactor
October 1952

My dear Sylvia, little wunderkind,
what a lovely story, no wonder it would win
the contest. I can hardly express
my pleasure, and I wish you the best

as you enter your third year at Smith.
I also write to inquire as to if
you might visit and talk over tea,
so delighted I'll be for your company.

You make an aging lady proud.
You are a writer avowed.
I have no doubt if you continue this way,
big publishing doors will open someday.

Olive Higgins Prouty lived in Brookline at 393 Walnut in a handsome two-story mansion. Sylvia visited Mrs. Prouty periodically throughout her life (in the early years once or twice a year when she was home on vacation from Smith), but their primary mode of communication was letters.

Tuberculosis

Dick Norton, Sylvia's on-and-off college boyfriend
Fall 1952, Sylvia's junior year

Heavy chest, fluid-filled,
they finally diagnose it correctly
and confine me to a sanatorium.

At least I have my blond, lovely,
bright-eyed Sylvia. I have decided
that she will be my wife.

I read her favorite authors:
Dylan Thomas, Thomas Mann,
the Russian novelists, so we can

engage in lively correspondence.
They plump me in this institution,
stuff me with medication and fortification.

I sometimes think that Sylvia
envies me, wishes to be seriously ill.
She fancies this is a retreat, a vacation

from responsibility. But my cough
pierces, deep as a samurai sword,
and I am profoundly alone.

I wish to agonize over a physical
science course like Sylvia, to escape
these white brick walls, this building

of small rooms. I am abundantly
grateful to have found the mother
of my children prior to contracting

TB. I am at present in no shape
to locate a life mate. My body softens
in these nurse-cornered sheets.

Only my resolve
of a future with Sylvia
remains firm.

Tuberculosis afflicted many medical students at this time. In the fifties, TB was
untreatable by medication, so those who were diagnosed with the disease were
required to be confined to a sanatorium for one to three years. The sanatorium
Dick recovered in was located at Saranac Lake, New York, in the Adirondack
Mountains.

Tendency to Overdramatize

Aurelia Plath
                    November–December 1952

Sivvy's letters of late
concern me. She questions
whether she should visit
the school psychiatrist,
checks herself into the infirmary again.

I can't ascertain whether
she is just tired, withered by
the dog gnawing at her heels.
Or if, like my ulcers, it is something
more. I tell her that

the semester is almost
at a close and things will improve.
I worry in silence that all
my scrimping and years
of secondhand clothes

may prove to be for naught,
frivoled away, underappreciated.
Sylvia longs for retreat like
the waves that have comforted her
since she was a baby.

I think she identifies with Dick,
believes she deserves escape
to a hospital bed, only she carries
no disease. I tell her mind
over matter, to garner her strength.

I reiterate that she is fine.
I promise that I will nurse her
back to health over Christmas break.

Sylvia's letters that so worried Aurelia (dated November 19 and December 15, 1952) can be found in *Letters Home: Correspondence 1950–1963*. Sylvia's descent into severe depression during this period is also chronicled in her published journals. Just before her Christmas break in 1952, Sylvia went to see a therapist at Smith.

Manic Depression

Imagining Sylvia Plath
          In the style of "Aerialist"
          December 1952

She balances night.
She floats on days.
She cannot see the shift—
Her smile of light,
Her frown of haze,
She's constantly adrift.

She breaks. She's sick.
Throw a rope, a net.
She falls like a shot-up plane.
Help her find the landing strip,
Her feet are wet—
She'll learn, she'll train.

She walks a rope on fire,
"Look Ma, no hands."
She falls with half-closed eyes.
She toils past her tire,
Exceeds demands,
She wins a golden prize.

She falls to earth.
Spends winters
Combing a mane of death.
She awaits spring's birth.
She splinters.
She's so knocked out of breath.

An acrobat of moods,
She juggles like a pro.
She clowns her painted lips.
She giggles. She broods.
She begs to be followed.
Then shifts and gives them all the slip.

"Aerialist" can be found in *The Collected Poems*.

The Caliber of Her Dating Pool

Myron "Mike" Lotz, another college boyfriend, roommate of Perry Nort
    (Dick's brother) at Yale
    December 1952

Even though I just met Sylvia,
we are so similar, two
snowflakes descending from
the same December sky,
light shimmering off our accolades—
her published stories and poems,
her editorial positions, balancing
my fast track to med school,
first in my class at Yale,
my recruitment by the Detroit Tigers.
And yet both of us keep these
things relatively quiet,
too polite to brag.

We look winning together.
Tall and lovely, we promenade
through the Smith campus
after her Lawrence House dance.
We pass the hospital, a patient's
wail rattles the glass windowpanes.
Sylvia twitches, something a little off.
She freezes, her pretty snowflake
halted midair. She can't fall to earth.
She hears the "Ooooooo" of the invalid
like he's a prisoner pleading for release,
and can't sleep.

She fascinates and enchants me,
but something seems amiss,
like the low murmur of clouds
moving in before it storms.
I hope Sylvia settles,
cascades to the ground, so we might
pile up together—
two crystals,
fighting against our ever-present heat.

Sylvia dated Mike, whom she called a "Hercules," but was also seriously enchanted with another boy, Gordon Lameyer, at this time. Sylvia became disillusioned with Mike after she visited him the weekend of May 9, 1953, at Yale. She found Mike to be insecure and overly obsessed with his own problems. Their relationship faded after that.

Ski Trip

Dick Norton, Sylvia's on-and-off college boyfriend
Late December 1952

When Sylvia cartwheeled
into the snowbank
she believed her fractured fibula
signified the end of us.

Sylvia pays for this symbol,
hobbles around campus for months,
recovers from her fall. Still bedridden,
I recover from the fall of us.

Sylvia does crazy things
to harm and sicken herself,
to extricate herself from situations
that frighten and exhaust her.

Sylvia treats me like a boring, ailing aunt.
She perplexes me, I am paper
perfect, what else could she want
in a mate? *Bonne chance!*

I hope she enjoys her hard-won
convalescence, and hope
she doesn't pray too hard that it lasts.
Sickness is a curse, not a cure.

When Sylvia visited Dick in the sanatorium over Christmas break 1952, she tried skiing for the first time. Dick was still very ill and laid up in bed, so Sylvia faced the slopes alone. She attempted a hill that was too advanced for her novice skills and broke her leg. An account of this incident appears in Sylvia's journals and in her novel, *The Bell Jar.*

Pretty, Tall, Crippled

Gordon Lameyer, a boy Sylvia dated in college
February 7, 1953

She descends the stairs
on crutches like a crippled
old man and I sigh, think,
Boy, this date's gonna be
loads of fun.

Sylvia speaks
as though she's unloading
an automatic rifle, one idea
shoots after another,
until every thought her mind holds
has been discharged
and she finds herself with nowhere to run.

My mother more or less
instigated this date,
so I expected Sylvia
to be pretty and intelligent,
and fairly dull.

But she shines
metallic. She admires me,
which, crutch or not,
jumps her a few stairs
in my estimation.

She writes letters
as though we will
get "pinned,"
as though fission
pulls us together.
"We'll see more of each other,"
I tell her.
We'll see,
I tell myself.

Gordon and Sylvia dated seriously from this meeting well into the summer of 1954. Sylvia was not, however, exclusive with him. When she became preoccupied with Richard Sassoon in November 1954, Gordon drifted from her love life.

Pleasure

Marybeth Little, Mademoiselle*'s College Board*
interviewer and judge
April 1953

We are pleased
to inform you
that you have won
a 1953 *Mademoiselle* guest editorship.
Please inform us
if you accept and will come to New York
for the month of June.

We are pleased
with you—
your decorum, your
fashion, your editorial
eye. You exemplify
the *Mademoiselle* girl.

We are pleased
to have you role model
and model our fall must-haves.
We think *you*
have that special something,
that "It" factor,
and, oh, you craft fine sentences too.

We are, after all,
pleased with you
but can't pay you much.
We'll connect you, put you in touch
with prominent writers,
New York culture, and men.
We'll house you at the Barbizon
Hotel. You have a bright future,
this we can tell.

We are pleased
to have you swell our staffs,
type copy, edit paragraphs.
Socialize and represent
the magazine's ethics and intent.

We are pleased, Sylvia,
please don't disappoint, Sylvia,
accept this appointment.
You are a star, Sylvia,
in the vast sky of American girls.
So be worthy, Sylvia,
of this stellar opportunity.

Twenty guest editors were selected each year, bright, ambitious women from the country's best colleges. *Mademoiselle* housed the girls in New York City's Barbizon Hotel for Women. Each girl was expected to write two articles for the magazine and perform editorial assistant duties, but one of the main goals of the program was to expose these young women to New York culture. They had very full and obligatory social calendars. The pay for the month's work was $150. Sylvia's guest editorship ran from June 1 to June 26, 1953.

Excellence

Cyrilly Abels, Managing Editor, Mademoiselle
June 1953

Impeccable.
Error free. On time.
I select Sylvia to be
my managing guest editor,
under my command.

I know
she can be pushed
to my standards.
Unlike the other girls
she rigors, a crossword

puzzler
who fills in all the blanks
correctly in blue ink,
no erasures. She sits
at her desk, changing

typewriter ribbons
after hours. Her Achilles'
heel that box of Kleenex
and those brown watery eyes,
but she holds her tears

around me.
I will suffer
none of these college girls
blubbering or blundering.
They are privileged,

must earn
their A+ status with me.
My hemline's exact,
cuticles clipped,
hair tucked smartly
behind my ears.

This magazine
is us. We must present.
I instill this in Sylvia.
She regards me
with glass eyes

and nods agreement.
She is accustomed
to a woman's high
expectations, to do
well by the family name.

She will make Plath
synonymous with greatness.
To be average
is to hibernate—
a lair neither I nor my staff
dare enter.

Mademoiselle Managing Editor Cyrilly Abels "was notorious for being immacu-
lately groomed, seriously intellectual, and she enjoyed close friendships with literary giants like Katherine Anne Porter and Dylan Thomas."—from *Rough Magic* by
Paul Alexander

Cyrilly Abels is the role model for Jay Cee in *The Bell Jar*. She and Sylvia stayed in
touch throughout Sylvia's life and would have lunch whenever Sylvia visited New
York City. Cyrilly published Sylvia's poem "Parallax," which won an honorable
mention in *Mademoiselle*'s 1954 Dylan Thomas poetry contest.

Stigmata

Janet Wagner, a fellow Mademoiselle *guest editor*
with whom Sylvia became friends
June 1953

Raised red bumps
that melded within a minute
into a crimson blush of shame,
a burning of the arms.

Sylvia feels the Rosenbergs'
electrocution as if they were relatives.
She burns with them, identifies
with spies. She eats nothing all day.

She stalks Dylan Thomas,
haunts his hangouts, but never
meets the man. She flings
her clothes, every garment

out the window of the Barbizon.
Asks me for an outfit
to wear on the train ride home.
I give her my old green dirndl skirt

and white peasant blouse
with eyelet ruffled sleeves.
She shoves her ratty blue
bathrobe into my arms. Insists

I take it. Tears spill
out of her eyes as she thrusts
the terry cloth at me
and she boards her train.

After that last New York
day, I never see Sylvia Plath again.

Janet Wagner is fictionalized in *The Bell Jar* primarily as the sweet, farm-fresh
Betsy from Kansas, but in reality she had a little bit of the more worldly Doreen
character in her as well. It is Betsy who gives the novel's lead character, Esther
Greenwood, clothes to wear home after Esther empties her suitcase out the hotel
window.

Home Bitter Home

Aurelia Plath
        June 1953

Grammy and I shift weight
heel to heel
on the platform.

We have been standing here
for over an hour
awaiting Sivvy's train.

Sylvia carries no baggage
but looks as though
her purse is filled with boulders.

No jaunt to her step, just a grimace
of resignation and relief
when she spies us. I erupt

into a pink, painted-on grin.
A vacancy blinks
behind her eyes like Sylvia's

checked herself into
a strange roadside motel
in the middle of nowhere,

surrounded by vagrants
but utterly alone. I smooth
her hair, but she's cold to my touch.

I must form my words
carefully. She fugues today,
lowered into a pit I recognize.

When I tell her
the summer fiction class
at Harvard is full,

she sees the transparency
of my words, that she was not
accepted.

She slumps into her blanket
of inadequacy. The summer air's
hot and foggy on the windows,

but our car ride home
rattles and freezes my bones.
Sylvia's backseat tears icicle to her face.

Sylvia's anguish over not being accepted into the summer fiction course Frank
O'Connor taught at Harvard is chronicled in her journal entry of July 6, 1953:
"You could be taking O'Connor's novel, etc.—but why blind yourself by taking
course after course: when if you are anybody, which you are no doubt not, you
should *not* be bored, but should be able to think, accept, *affirm*—and not retreat
into a masochistic mental hell where jealousy and fear make you want to stop
eating. . . ."

Stalemate

Dick Norton, Sylvia's on-and-off college boyfriend
July 1953

Sylvia makes me sadder
than my TB.

Stymied like a fly
stuck in amber, she writes

that she cannot write,
confides in her mother

that her muse has retired,
abandoned her, left her

with no imagination, just
nerve ends of worry.

Unquiet swarms
her brain. She gallivants

about New York City,
dines at 21 with the literary elite,

but cannot endure
a single blemish—her skin

is that sensitive.
Not being accepted

into Harvard summer school
makes her feel as though

her whole face is marred.
She may know real pain

one day and appreciate
how good she has it.

I fret for Sylvia.
She appears anchored

to the idea of sinking,
which is silly when she so clearly

soars above almost everyone.
Still, inertia withers

the bones. I know this too well.
I advise her to break her stasis.

Dick and Sylvia were writing letters to each other at this time.

Shock Treatment

Aurelia Plath
>*July 29, 1953*

I hold my baby in my arms,
her legs scarred by razor
just to test if she had the nerve
to drag the blade across her skin.

She begs me to die with her.
I schedule Sylvia an appointment
with a psychiatrist. He suggests
we shock her out of depression.

Metal probes attach
to her forehead. She is rigid,
alone in that room, prostrate
on the table, but we follow

the doctor's orders. I will not
be foolish with Sylvia as I was
with Otto. We will seek out
and listen to medical professionals

before it is too late.
Sylvia doesn't sleep. A return
to infancy, she cries and wakes
in the night. I lock her sleeping pills

away, distribute them judiciously,
as prescribed, even though Sylvia
begs for more. Sylvia's electrified—
pills or no pills, she struggles to shut her eyes.

These initial shock treatments were prescribed by Dr. J. Peter Thornton and administered at Valley Head Hospital. Electroshock therapy was considered, at the time, to be effective in alleviating emotional distress.

Suicide Watch

Warren Plath
August 24–27, 1953

Sylvia has shielded herself
with a coffin lid as long as
I can remember. She vampires

under full moon, sleeps fifteen
hours or not a wink. My sister
of extremes, shifty as the moon,

Syl suns herself beachside
or rots in a dark cupboard.
She scares us like kids

on Halloween, wants to ghost
this home instead of live in it.
She leaves a note that she has gone

for a long walk and will return
tomorrow. But Mother knows better,
the lockbox of sleeping pills smashed.

Ambulance lights swirl our brains.
We phone the police, report her missing.
It seems to me Sylvia has been missing

since she returned from New York.
The neighbors scour the fields
with flashlights and hound dogs.

The headlines report *Beautiful
Smith Girl Missing.* Then Grammy
hears it—scuffle and moan,

like a large rodent in the cellar.
Thump from behind the wood stack.
I remove logs and panel

and find Sylvia swaddled
in a blanket, covered in vomit.
Her cheek bloody, she is blue-lipped,

blue-fingertipped, her skin pallid
purple. I feel her exhale on my palm
and carry her to the ambulance.

She nearly nailed herself
in this time, burrowed
into her wooden death box.

But the ghosts refuse her,
not enough room in this house
for another apparition.

Our father's presence lingers.
Thank God I found Sylvia, that
on the third day she rises.

I pray that she recovers.
Sylvia's illness weighs heavy on my back.
I grow weary, like Atlas shouldering the world.

How many times can I carry Sylvia to safety?
I do not want to lose my only sibling.
Our family's stability hinges on her presence.

Sylvia's novel, The Bell Jar, is a fictional account of this suicide attempt. The
Boston Globe, the Boston Herald, and the Boston Post all ran stories about Sylvia's
disappearance and recovery. That Sylvia attempted suicide was not mentioned in
these accounts.

August 1953

Imagining Sylvia Plath
    In the style of "The Fearful"

Her summer is a winter—
Frostbite, gangrene that devours her inside out.

Her wintering is a glass bell—
Frozen crystal tongue without tingle, without chime.

Her glass bell suffocates fireflies, honeybees,
Jars them in heat, turns off their little minds.

Her fireflies must be shocked, relit.
Depression oozes from her fingers, softens her brain.

Her brain quiets under the cupboard.
She presses herself inside a wooden cellar box.

The cupboard is a faulty coffin—too many
Breathing holes won't let her be snuffed out.

She broke her mother's locked box
Of pills and swallowed them all.

Broke her mother's heart, but her stomach
Saves her, betrays her, won't keep death down.

More dead than alive, they found her
Blue-lipped but breathing, three days later.

"The Fearful" was written November 16, 1962. It is included in the Pulitzer Prize–winning *The Collected Poems*. A less well-known poem, certain lines in "The Fearful" link to the same drive toward suicide Sylvia struggled with not only in November 1962 but also back in 1953. For example:

The voice of the woman hollows—
More and more like a dead one,

Aid

Olive Higgins Prouty
August 27–28, 1953

Read in paper about Sylvia, stop.
I offer her assistance, stop.
No worries about money,
I'll finance her recovery, stop.

Broke down once myself, stop.
Understand how low one drops.
Have great doctors to recommend.
Syl will be stitched up, will mend.
She will never do this again, stop.

Olive Higgins Prouty paid for all of Sylvia's medical expenses. She even convinced doctors and hospitals to reduce or waive their fees. Prouty sent money and aid to Sylvia throughout Sylvia's life, not only for medical expenses but to help support Sylvia as a writer. Olive Higgins Prouty is fictionalized as Philomene Guinea in *The Bell Jar*. Chapter fifteen describes the events of the poem above.

Doctor-Patient Relations: Trial and Error

Dr. Lindemann, Massachusetts General Hospital
September 1953

I diagnosed her
with adolescent nervous illness,
not the black smudge of mental disease—
perhaps I was wrong?

Miss Plath doesn't take to the ward.
Like a child in after-school detention,
it's as though she'd rather be set on fire
than retained here. She should animate,
not vegetate, at this stage of recovery.
What's wrong with her?

In group, I expose her to patients
who have never approached the door
marked "normal." I had hoped Miss Plath
would find gratitude, realize that her situation
is not so dire. But she retires further into herself.
I have done this all wrong.

I want to help her get well.
I believe that I may be
the wrong doctor for Sylvia.
But wrong as I am,
will anyone be right?

Sylvia was examined by Olive Higgins Prouty's psychiatrist, Dr. Donald McPherson, and by Dr. Erich Lindemann, the head of Massachusetts General Hospital's psychiatric wing. Then at McLean Hospital, a part of the Massachusetts General system (McLean was considered at the time to be one of the country's best mental facilities), Sylvia was cared for by Dr. Ruth Beuscher. Sylvia was at Massachusetts General from September 3, 1953, until no later than September 28, 1953. The patients were segregated strictly by gender and no other criteria, so many of the residents surrounding Sylvia were extremely mentally ill.

Doctor's Notes

Dr. Ruth Beuscher, Sylvia's lifelong psychiatrist
Fall 1953

Sylvia slumps on the couch,
neither lying nor sitting,
uncomfortable in her sweater set.
Her scarred cheek still decides
whether or not it will heal itself.

I remember the boiling teapot
of pressure attending the Ivy League
produced—those days only a few
years in my past. I relate
to Sylvia, must be careful,

must find a way to help her
without falling into a vortex myself.
I believe we can salve her demons together.
If she can begin to trust me,
perhaps she'll learn to trust herself.

My two little ones, my divorce,
my express imperative to be
a professional woman and a wife
and a mother. She observes how
I roll my sleeves, and next session

she has cuffed them exactly like mine.
I reveal myself to her, diary page by diary page,
watch pale Sylvia attain a soft rose
blush, silent but connecting
to me.

I think Sylvia will teach me
at least as much as I teach her.
The question is, what will we learn?

Dr. Ruth Tiffany Barnhouse Beuscher was assigned as Sylvia's personal psychiatrist at McLean. McLean was a teaching hospital, and Ruth was a psychiatric resident. When Sylvia began psychotherapy sessions with Ruth, Mrs. Prouty and Aurelia did not know that Ruth was a novice therapist. In a letter Ruth wrote to Sylvia, she once said, "I have often thought, if I 'cure' no one else in my whole career, you are enough. I love you. Good luck—Ruth B." Sylvia's death so shook Dr. Beuscher, she underwent therapy and divorced her second husband.

Abecedarian

Wilbury Crockett, Sylvia's high school English teacher
        Fall 1953

Absent as a
bear in deep winter, her mind
can't connect, her memory appears
dead. Her ace brain has switched off.
Everyone worries for Sylvia.
For me the tragedy is acute. I refuse to
give up on her. I bring
her Scrabble letters. Arrange them
into simple words, AN or TAN, attempt to
jolt her mind into memory, into the
kinetic world. I grasp her finger—move the
letters to form the conjunctive AND.
My star pupil, my friend—
never could I imagine that words would become
obsolete, inaccessible, a
puzzle her mind can't
quite solve. I
resist my impulse to
spell for her. Her brittle fingers
touch the letters foreign as braille.
Unlock the language, Sylvia, please. What
violence in her mind caused this?
Who will she be without words? An
X on her forehead where they shocked her
yellow and purple and black.
Zealots every one of them, under medicine's reckless thumb.

Sylvia's hands tremble. She pushes the letters,
slow as an hour hand.
She looks up at me with an almost smile.
The word on the table is THANKS.
Now I tremble; never in my academic career
have I been prouder.

An abecedarian is a poetry form in which each of the twenty-six lines either ends
or begins with the sequential letters of the alphabet. In the poem above, the lines
begin alphabetically. Mr. Crockett visited McLean Hospital once a week for the
five months that Sylvia was there.

Debate

Nurse at McLean Hospital/Sanatorium
Fall 1953

You hear 'em all bicker
like an alley of hungry cats,
not really in a claw fight
but each of them wanting
to outscreech the other.

Poor thing, that Sylvia,
lies in bed like a coma victim,
like she don't know where she is
most days. Everything hazy and half-lit
to her. While they jabber
over insulin treatments, head-shrinkin',
which little pills
I should drop into her cup,
she barely blinks. They whisper
that they might strap her
to that shock table
we call Frankenstein's bed.

Poor child's mother—
thank goodness my Libby
ain't holed up in here.
I ache for these trembling
little girls with slashed wrists,
their minds stranded
at the side of the road.
Don't know what I'd do
with all these doctors purring
at my heels, scratching my leg
to get their way. I'd want to lift
my baby out of this white-walled crib.
Guess in the end, that's what they all want.

McLean was a private mental facility in Belmont but part of the Massachusetts General system. The hospital offered pleasant surroundings, individualized attention, and the most advanced techniques. Electroshock therapy and psychotherapy were used to treat suicide and psychotic episodes. Daily insulin treatments and long periods of unstructured free time in which Sylvia could elect to engage in occupational therapy were prescribed for Sylvia by Dr. Beuscher. Mrs. Prouty complained that this form of therapy was isolating and bad for Sylvia.

Sylvia was first diagnosed by Dr. Lindemann with an adolescent nervous illness, from which she was told she would recover fully. He believed that Sylvia suffered no mental disease or psychosis. Dr. McPherson diagnosed Sylvia as having had an acute schizophrenic episode, which at the time meant that Sylvia had suffered a period of disassociation from which patients usually emerged. Dr. Beuscher treated Sylvia for depression leading to suicidal tendencies.

Madness

Dr. Beuscher, Sylvia's therapist
       Fall 1953

Repression cuts off
circulation like a tourniquet,
and Sylvia throbs with desire.

I advise Sylvia to experiment,
to stop fretting over a white
wedding dress. Does this shock
the patient? Not really.
Sylvia has been slicing at her arm,
waiting for someone
to grant her permission.

A junior in college,
she may be ready for this.
"But what would Mother think?"
Sylvia snickers. She wraps a mink stole
of secrets around her shoulders,
luxuriates in playing foul
behind her mother's back.

Perhaps when she holds back
her desires, her mind
splinters into madness, into deadwood
that we must burn away by electric shock.
I encourage her to release her idea
of the bad girl, punishable for physical contact.
I ask her to think about herself, not her mother,
about how Sylvia represses Sylvia.
I want to tell her to do what she wants.
I need to help her to let go of her fears.

Dr. Beuscher met with Sylvia for daily psychotherapy sessions, during which the doctor explained to Sylvia her methods and techniques and why she was using them. Sylvia responded well to this sort of inclusion and respect. Dr. Beuscher employed fairly orthodox Freudianism, which entailed leading analysis and discussions about Sylvia's childhood. At the time of the above poem, Sylvia and Ruth met at McLean Hospital for inpatient treatment, but later they would have sessions at Dr. Beuscher's private practice. They were in weekly contact via phone or letters, or in person, until Sylvia's death ten years later.

Oxymoron

Warren Plath
        January 1954

The road piled in snow.
The windows a slimy fog.
I wasn't speeding, but the car
hit a patch of black ice
slick as baby oil
and we might have plunged eternal
into Paradise Pond,
except that I did right,
turned hard into the skid.
My knuckles blue, I held the steering
wheel so tight.

We missed the pines.
We avoided the rocks.
The street was a ghost town,
no other fools suffering travel
in that weather. We collided
with an embankment, a soft jolt
backward like hitting a bumper
during a crash test.

Sivvy clawed the dashboard.
Her eyes closed
as if to welcome death.
She trembled
the rest of the drive to Smith.
She never blamed me, exactly,
anyone might have lost control
of the car, but I could hear
in her thank you, her goodbye,
that she will likely never ride
passenger with me again.

She did not want to drive
into her death. Pill herself
to long sleep, maybe—
but to die at the hand
of ice and motorized sheet metal
and my mismanaged driving,
Sylvia would not be subject
to that or any epitaph she didn't script.

Sylvia missed only one semester at Smith, the fall of what would have been her
senior year. She took a lightened course load when she returned to Smith at the
beginning of 1954, and this caused her to have to attend another full senior year,
fall 1954 through spring 1955.

Blond Ambition

Nancy Hunter, Sylvia's friend
        and later roommate at Smith
        Winter 1954

She bottles her hair white gold
so she radiates among the crowds.

She types her way back to health,
click-clack of keys, composing her own words,

not secretary to her mentor's
manuscript. She types to be heard,

and when she calls out into the cave
of the *Smith Review* and *Harper's Magazine*

the editors echo back, "Yes, Yes."
She wears celebrity well, known as

the campus Lazarus, back from the dead. She has seen
the other side, now an entourage swarms her feet.

She confides to me in the dark hours—
that stagnant swell before dawn,

that she took the pills to erase tedium—
that precursor to depression's quicksand.

She says she killed her father—wished him dead
when she was a little girl,

and when he obliged, it was like she
had strangled a part of herself.

A heavy chain of guilt threatens
to pull her into drowning at any time.

And last August she became too tired to swim.
Lethargy, inertia, the stagnant water over her head.

Sylvia and Nancy roomed together at Lawrence House during Sylvia's senior year at Smith, from 1954 to 1955. After college, they kept in touch and remained friends.

Golden Girl

Richard Sassoon, roommate of two other boys Sylvia dated,
one of her great love affairs
Spring 1954

Golden girl,
Neck of pearl,
Sylvia dates us all.

Statuesque, a pall
Around her edge,
She constructs herself

Out of typewriter ribbon,
Takes it as a given
That men fall

One after the other,
Spelled by her talk,
Her golden locks,

Her little shocks,
They're just domino blocks
She knocks down.

I ask if she'll accompany me
To New York City,
She agrees.

For what I foresee
Is a future where Sylvia
Falls for me.

Richard Sassoon was related to Siegfried Sassoon, an acclaimed English poet of the
Great War generation.

Twins

*Nancy Hunter, Sylvia's friend and roommate at Smith
Summer 1954*

Sylvia feeds off my leftovers.
I toss Edwin curbside
after a night of skirting around
the divan, escaping his advances.

Most girls would run from this sort
of brute, move out of the way
of Edwin's falling anvil.
But Sylvia reviled

and then followed after Edwin.
Almost magnetized, she accepted
his calls and dinner invitations,
only to feel buyer's remorse.

He cut her, the bastard,
ripped her during intercourse
so that blood like lava
gushed between her legs.

Sylvia said it was her first time.
When the bleeding wouldn't stop,
I took her to the hospital for repair,
forced the little weasel to drive us there.

He said he'd check on Sylvia tomorrow,
but I knew his intentions
were fake promissory notes.
I wanted to spit on his trench coat,

dunk his big head in a vat of tar
and roll him in dirt,
but instead I told him
not to bother calling.

I protect my Sylvia and she watches
after me. I will stop her from jumping
in front of trains, even if I have to bind
my own hands and feet to the rail.

The author Ronald Hayman asserts in his *The Death and Life of Sylvia Plath* that Nancy felt that Sylvia sometimes counted on "crises to give her creative inspiration," and that "for the sake of her poetry and her stories she [took] risks and [depended] on other people to rescue her from dangerous situations."

Marriage

Gordon Lameyer, a boy Sylvia dated in college
August 1954

Sylvia sings,
not angelic, but like a Mozart
recording, comfortable, well listened to,
a few scratches on the LP so the record
jumps about but always settles into beauty.

Her hand in mine—
she, the proverbial key opening my lock.
I tell her I will hold her hand forever,
do not fear pregnancy,
do not conceive of maternity

as a trapdoor one can't squirm out of,
but rather as a portal to safety
and security, to a room in the adult world.
We are adults, after all.

Bridesmaid at her friend Marcia's
wedding, Sylvia stands near the altar.
Why then is she so afraid?
Syl tells me I am the one,
that she loves me.

I resound, "Yes, Yes,"
like something out of a Joyce novel,
but Sylvia switches her senior thesis
from the Irishman
to exploring literary doubles in Dostoevsky
and other men.

Sylvia feared marriage at this time because she struggled over the question of how one can be an artist devoted to her work and a wife and mother. In August 1954 Sylvia worried that she had become pregnant by Gordon, and she did not want to be forced into marriage because of an untimely pregnancy. It turned out that Sylvia was not pregnant.

Sylvia's struggles over the question of marriage and how to reconcile that with her need to be an artist fill her journal pages.

Sylvia's original senior thesis was on James Joyce, but she switched it to a study of Dostoevsky's novels *The Double* and *The Brothers Karamazov*, specifically examining Dostoevsky's use of dual images and characters that mirror one another. The subject was personal for Sylvia because it reflected her awareness of her own divided and tumultuous nature.

Iconic

A freshman at Smith
Fall 1954

There she is, Sylvia Plath,
Books in tow, lips red and chapped.

See the scar, dark under her eye—
She tried to off herself, I'm not sure why.

So lovely and published, a star in Smith's sky.
If I had all she has, I wouldn't want to die.

They follow her like a herd of geese,
Ladies lunching at her knees.

I might do so too, show her who I am.
But like the Golden Girl I'm not a lamb.

Hearsay tells she charms many men.
They fall like rain, not content to be friend.

She squirrels about, her many trees to tend.
Then climbs high branches that never end.

Sylvia did not appear particularly burdened or embarrassed by the public knowledge of her suicide attempt and hospitalization. Her incident allowed her certain privileges—a lightened school schedule, fewer chores, and a private room in her dorm, Lawrence House. Sylvia continued to be an exceptional student, and she was treated with awe and esteem. In some ways, Sylvia seemed to like the attention.

Recommendation

Estella Kelsey, Sylvia's senior-year housemother
at her dormitory, Lawrence House
Fall 1954

Clack–clack–clack–ding,
all hours of night and day,
Sylvia rings our ears
with her typewriting machine,
as though her words
are more vital than our sleep.

The vocational office informs me
that I am to write Sylvia
a letter of recommendation
so that she might be awarded
a Fulbright scholarship.

Well, tish, I clackety–click
out my statement of truth.
Talented as a well–bred
racehorse and just about as spoiled,
Sylvia runs around this place
as though she is a guest author in residence.

More seasoned than the other girls,
they best not block Sylvia's path
to the finish line. I select my words,
type the letter straight. I do understand
Sylvia needs money. But she also needs
to find some gratitude.

Smith was an all-women's college, and Lawrence House was a dormitory specifically for girls on scholarship, wherein house duties and chores helped to defray their room-and-board expenses. A housemother lived in the dormitory with the students and was charged with overseeing the girls and making sure that the dorm rules were upheld.

Darling, Darling

Richard Sassoon, one of Sylvia's great love affairs
1955

I chide you,
whisk you off to New York.
We feast on theater,
savor art like fine cabernet.
Gorge ourselves
on each other's lips
as though each kiss
were the necessary antidote
to our separation.

You turn
from everybody's good-time girl
into a butterfly
caught in my silver net,
content to light on my chest.
I become your sun,
your nectar.
You flap against my web,
yet are grateful to be confined.

I take you in hand
when you try to fly away
and amuse yourself
on another wind.
Sylvia, you must
land. You desire this,
to be held in place.
You need me
to fashion your cocoon.

Sylvia became disillusioned with Richard in 1955 as she completed her senior
year at Smith. Part of her loss of interest was because Richard appeared to have
fallen overly in love with her. Nevertheless, Richard is the one who ultimately
broke the relationship off and left Sylvia heartbroken.

Bragging Rights

Aurelia Plath
        June 1955

My little Sivvy graduates,
a briefcase of accolades
to bolster her into higher learning.

She surpasses me. Her reading
list above my skill set.
This has been my dream,

and yet my stomach flares
like a dynamite stick. It explodes,
requires repair, keeps me from my dear.

I open letter after letter.
Sylvia wins the Glascock Poetry
competition, publishes

in the *Christian Science Monitor,*
Mademoiselle, and
the *Atlantic Monthly.*

They award my daughter
the Christopher Prize,
the Alpha Phi Kappa Psi award,

the Alpha Creative Writing award,
the Elizabeth Babcock Poetry Prize.
Sivvy judges literary festivals.

She wins or places in almost
everything she enters. She sends
me her ribbons and placards,

they collect on my wall
like a montage of success.
I store the surplus in a cedar chest.

The prize money she retains.
The phone beside my hospital bed
buzzes and quivers, Sylvia's voice

trills higher than the Wellesley water tower.
She has been awarded a Fulbright
to study at Cambridge.

I elevate my bed, bubble up
out of my stomachache stupor,
tell her I am exceedingly proud of her.

Our toils paid off.
When I hang up the receiver
and lower myself back to horizontal,

my expression concaves.
Sylvia will live an ocean away—
move beyond my sight and reach.

I try to smile about this departure.
I will travel on a mattress
in the back of Marian's station wagon

to watch Sivvy accept her diploma.
And then I must wave her off across the Atlantic,
watch her ship slide quickly beyond my grasp.

Sylvia graduated on June 6, 1955, at the age of twenty-two. Aurelia was recovering from a subtotal gastrectomy.

Put Your Studies to Good Use

Adlai Stevenson, Smith 1955 commencement address

Impressive what you
girls accomplished at Smith, but now
you must pursue your

highest vocation—
achieve a creative marriage,
thrive beside a man.

Despite the sentiments expressed above, presidential candidate Stevenson was
thought to be a progressive politician.

Farewell, Boys

Warren Plath
September 1955

Her boat departs for England
and Sylvia releases the sailor knot
that kept her safely docked in Boston Harbor.

She ends her affair
with Peter Davison, that young
editor at Harvard University Press

she seemed so enchanted with
just last week. It's as though Peter
were a summer head scarf

and as the season passes, he's
not worth packing. She seals
the envelope with Gordon too,

lipstick prints goodbyed
over the adhesive. She wants
no loose strings on her London-

worthy cloak. Richard Sassoon
puzzles her. As the *Queen Elizabeth*
steams away from shore,

Richard becomes smaller
and smaller, almost insignificant.
Almost as if he were never standing

on shore at all. And then
there is me, the one constant
male in her saltwater.

I drive her to the ship, witness
the men come and go
with her shifting winds.

I wave, blow her a kiss.
My sister, soon to be a Brit.
I want her to fare well.

In the fall of 1953 Warren was a junior at Harvard.

American Girl

Mrs. Milne, housemother at Whitstead, Sylvia's dormitory at Cambridge/Newnham College Fall 1955

She's a wee bit different
from the other girls,
cuts her eggs into squares.

She lets her male "friend"
use the ladies' loo. I saw him
tiptoe into a stall at dawn.

When I scold Sylvia,
tell her that this is not proper,
she eyes me with those big browns

as though I'm the foolhardy.
"Why not?" She presses me
like a linen shirt.

I rap on the metal canister
where ladies deposit napkins.
"They don't have these

on the bottom floor
and we don't have men
on the top."

The U.S. Fulbright Scholar Program, the U.S. government's flagship program in international educational exchange, was proposed to the U.S. Congress in 1945 by freshman senator J. William Fulbright of Arkansas. The Fulbright Program sends 800 scholars and professionals each year to more than 140 countries, where they lecture or conduct research in a wide variety of academic and professional fields.

The University of Cambridge is one of the oldest universities in the world and one of the largest in the United Kingdom. Cambridge has a worldwide reputation for outstanding academic achievement by its students.

Duplicate

Jane Baltzell, another American student attending
Cambridge/Newnham and residing at Whitstead
Fall 1955

We bike into town to dine.
Sylvia sports her *Mademoiselle*
casual couture. She rah-rahs
her American accent like a pom-pom girl.

I flush embarrassed when she taps
a young man on the shoulder,
wonders if he might recommend
a very British, very picturesque place to eat.

We are students, not tourists.
Sylvia assimilates about as well
as a hog snorting through
a field of fillies.

They branded us the American twins,
both of us tall and blond.
We could trade skirts, though nothing
in my bureau suits Sylvia's taste,

and vice versa. "There may not be
enough room in this English program
for the two of us," Sylvia laughs.
But we both know her jest contains truth.

Jane Baltzell Kopp was recorded at her Arkansas home in November 1973 responding to questions from Edward Butscher on these experiences.

Jane Baltzell Kopp went on to translate the *Poetria nova* into English. This has been done by only two other people. The *Poetria nova* is a thirteenth-century instructive treatise invented by Geoffrey of Vinsauf, which gives specific advice to future writers about the composition of poetry. The text itself serves as an illustration of the techniques it teaches.

My Notes on the Renowned Miss Plath's Submission

John Lehmann, editor at the London Magazine
1955

Unimpressed. I say
you're frightened to feel, create
mice where should be rats.

Two poems in the batch Sylvia submitted to the *London Magazine* were "Dance Macabre" and "Ice Age," both of which can be found in *The Collected Poems*. Sylvia published many poems and stories in the *London Magazine* later in life, including "The Applicant," one of the three *Ariel* poems accepted before she died.

Self-Centered

Mallory Wober, Sylvia's British boyfriend
her first semester at Cambridge
Fall 1955

Sylvia swishes
into King's College dining hall,
removes her exterior gloves,
and twenty heads twist
away from the orchestra,
aroused not by sound
or any of the regular five senses,
but drawn to her essence.

She's accustomed
to this sort of response,
a silent queen of the bees,
she understands her import
in the hive, produces well
to retain her status. Sylvia charms
us mortals with her poems
and her ball gowns.

I shake off my outer coat
and, like a happy drone,
guide the royal
to her seat.

Sylvia met Mallory at a Labour Party dance. A fellow student, Mallory was more exotic than other British men because he had lived in India. When Sylvia studied at Cambridge, men outnumbered women ten to one!

Love Affair

Richard Sassoon, one of Sylvia's great loves
December 1955

Paris whirls blue and
dark blue. Sylvia begins and
ends me, belongs here.

A beautiful account of Sylvia's travels with Richard during December 1955 and January 1956 can be found in the appendix of *The Journals of Sylvia Plath: 1950–1962*. On this vacation, Richard danced Sylvia around all the famous sights of Paris. They spent Christmas morning on the steps of Notre Dame Cathedral. Sylvia grew to love Paris even more than London.

As she packed her bags to return to Cambridge, Richard told Sylvia he intended to see other women and they had a terrible fight. This visit would be the last significant time they spent together.

Overreaction

Jane Baltzell, another American student at Cambridge,
      Sylvia's doppelgänger, with whom she traveled to Paris
      December 1955

Sylvia raged, rain-drenched,
dagger eyes.
I'd locked her out,
poor culpable me.

Jane and Sylvia were more or less forced to travel together. Due to bad weather, all planes into Paris were grounded, so the girls instead took a ferry across stormy waters, bonding as they sipped brandy together under Jane's raincoat and attempted to avoid seasickness. As they arrived too late for Jane to check into a hotel, Sylvia let Jane stay in her room. Despite the late hour and bad weather, Sylvia wanted to go out that night and explore. But Jane was exhausted and collapsed into bed, sleeping so soundly she did not hear Sylvia banging on the door to be let in. Jane had also left the key in the lock after she locked the door from the inside, so even the concierge with his master key could not let Sylvia into her room. Sylvia and Jane's friendship was delicate, and Sylvia was furious beyond reason. The episode was peaceably resolved by Jane's agreement to be more responsible with the key. When Jane left Paris for Italy a few days later, she locked the key in the room a second time.

Paris in the Winter

Imagining Sylvia Plath
> *In the style of "Winter Landscape, with Rooks"*
> *Winter 1956*

She repeats his name like a lullaby,
    the sonorous Sassoon. He sings
to her, then flaps his wings, a magpie
    shaking his tail of her. Nothing
for her between his beak except lies.

She sketched this out in faded watercolor,
    Richard not answering
her bell, fleeing her like a schoolboy. Where
    did he run? She circles his building.
She taps her toes. Did he even open her letter?

She freezes this trip to Paris, the city of pigeons.
    There are not enough scarves to warm her.
She stalks his door. She awaits his return,
    ridiculous as a rook without its jacket of feathers.
She never once glimpses his silhouette against the curtain.

"Winter Landscape, with Rooks" is the second poem in *The Collected Poems*. Sylvia
wrote about this poem in her journal, February 20, 1956: "Wrote one good poem:
'Winter Landscape, with Rooks': it moves, and is athletic: a psychic landscape."

St. Botolph's Party: Meeting Sylvia Plath

Ted Hughes, poet, Sylvia's future husband
February 25, 1956

I may be black panther
but she draws blood,
swirls whiskey-headed
around the dance floor,
dizzy on my poetry.

Her mind traps my lines
with the proficiency
I quote Shakespeare's.
She adores my words,
whispers that I will be
part of the pantheon.

I yank this Sylvia Plath
into a room of desk
and books, out of range
of the girl-of-the-moment
I brought to the party.

Blond and tall as a magazine
swimsuit model. I nibble
at the whippet's neck.
Her lips fury-red, she bites
me—teeth tearing my cheek.
I retreat, imprinted, stunned.

The party for our little
lit mag rages, wine-soaked,
behind the mahogany door.
Sylvia jets from the room.
She has tasted me. Her mouth is full.

I touch the blood on my face.
Will I ever be the same?

At the time Sylvia met Ted Hughes, he was no longer attending Cambridge, just hanging around the university discussing poetry and politics and establishing the short-lived literary magazine *St. Botolph's Review*. Ted was renowned as one of the best poets within the university community, even though he had published very little—a few poems in *Delta* and *Chequer*. Although Ted wrote a lot of poetry during this period, including one of his most anthologized poems, "The Jaguar," he simply did not vigorously pursue publication.

Germany

Gordon Lameyer, one of Sylvia's old boyfriends
April 1956

Last-ditch effort
to make fire of our
romantic embers, but we find
no phoenix in the ash.

We should spark flint
into friendship, but when Sylvia
rants that John Malcolm Brinnin
could have/should have saved

that old Welsh hero of hers,
Dylan Thomas, sad overrated
"dying of the light" poet that he is,
I will not concede to her.

Sylvia dials up the volume
of her argument, pounds
the alehouse table. I proffer
that Brinnin could never stop Thomas

from Thomas's inevitable,
predestined, predetermined
march toward self-destruction.
Sylvia eyes me, brimstone mad.

I almost hit below the belt
and argue that she of all people
should understand this,
for like her favorite poet

no one can stop Sylvia
when she holds a knife
to her throat. Only the one
who grips the handle can lower the blade.

John Malcolm Brinnin was an American poet and biographer, probably best known for his personal memoir *Dylan Thomas in America*. Brinnin brought Thomas, a Welsh poet, to America and accompanied him on his reading tours. Dylan Thomas loved to carouse and misbehave, and was an outspoken, foul-mouthed alcoholic. The implication in the above poem is that Brinnin, as one of Thomas's close friends, should have gotten Thomas help, not enabled his destructive behavior. Lots of controversy surrounds Thomas's death, but whether he drank himself into a stupor and then slipped into a coma or a doctor gave him a medical overdose that induced a coma, Thomas was destroying himself with alcohol and drugs and reckless behavior. The medical record cites pneumonia as the cause of Dylan Thomas's death.

Theodore

Imagining Sylvia Plath
In the style of "Ode for Ted"
April 1956

She loves that he names the trees,
all the creatures and leaves
of the forest and fen, receives
his knowledge like a corsage,
never has she known a man so large;
she believes he's her Adam and she's his Eve.

When she first drank his blood,
she knew no other man would taste so good;
knew what coursed his veins could
kill her. He dwarfed her previous lovers
with his talent and his hands. Only her father
was a figure so grand, a bard of the land, a druid.

She twirls around him on tiptoes,
polishes her lines like leather shoes;
he wears her on his lapel like a blue rose—
a cut flower weathering drought, she withstands
the squinty eyes of his poet friends,
is she worthy of Mr. Hughes?

Evangelical about his words, his worth,
she will spread his poems like fine marmalade, birth
his name to greatness, expand him breadth and width;
she breathes Ted, feeds and writes
him; they dream each other day and night;
she feels like the moon, a muse, orbiting Ted's earth.

"Ode for Ted" was written April 21, 1956, about Ted Hughes when Sylvia and Ted were courting and falling in love. Ted had an extensive knowledge of indigenous flora and could identify most countryside plants. "Ode for Ted" is a tribute to that skill of his and to his rugged, masculine character. Ted and Sylvia met in February 1956. They were married June 16, 1956, less than five months later.

Falling in Love with America

Ted Hughes, poet, Sylvia's future husband
May 1956

She is grand. She is
literature. She is beauty.
She masks a vast brain

under her blondness,
but when she reads her poems,
her great sheaf of verse,

I see genius. She
has been netting words longer
than I. She ignites

my writing like gales
spread forest fire. We sit
without a comma

of breath between us.
Her hands cup my face and I
devote everything

to her, move closer
to Cambridge, dream her thick lips,
her native tongue, her

language on the verge
of immortal. She's hungry.
She needs to be fed.

Most men can't handle
Sylvia's banging of plates.
Her appetite for

blood, poetry, sex.
But I am spun. She gives me
a new world, new words.

Edward James Hughes (Ted) was born on August 17, 1930, in Mytholmroyd, an English village in the narrow cleft of the Yorkshire Pennines. Ted had never been to America when he met Sylvia.

June Wedding

Aurelia Plath
June 1956

I could not predict,
did not expect,
that only three days

on the Isle of Britain
I would play witness
as Sylvia gives her hand

to this Ted Hughes
she mentioned in a few letters
and whom I have just met.

I smile, iron the pink knit
suit I bought myself,
give it to my daughter

to wear as a bridal gown.
Sivvy vows her love to this Ted,
embraces his life of poetry and poverty.

I smile, my teeth tremor
behind my lips. I wished an easier
life for Sylvia, a doctor or lawyer

to support her as she creates
writing and children. But Sivvy
is not a child anymore—

she traveled an ocean, put
that much salt water between us
and then did as she wanted.

I never could control her tides
or her will. I hug Ted.
My arms wrap awkwardly

around the back of this tall
man that I must now call
my son.

Sylvia and Ted were married in London near Queen's Square in the Church of St. George the Martyr at one-thirty in the afternoon on June 16, 1956. Ted had purchased the marriage license from the Archbishop of Canterbury that morning. They told no one except Aurelia, who was their only guest, that they were getting married. The curate stood as second witness.

Benidorm

Ted Hughes, Sylvia's husband
July–August 1956

Spanish honeymoon on half a farthing.
The harbor at Angel's Bay salivates
my pen and I am hungry for words
to capture this scenery, to snare
the maiden flight of our love.

I am not sentimental,
but when Sylvia sketches the rock cliffs
in precise ink lines, I am grateful
she traps our memories. Our daily fish
and fruit, the French doors open to sea

as we roll nightly under covers
and stars. This union explodes,
dangerous but irresistible.
I school Sylvia, prescribe daily
writing exercises, set our schedule

by the clock of the sun.
We discipline ourselves to a life
of poetry. I cannot breathe
any other way. My Sylvia is an A student,
she toils away, hopes that someday

her work will be on a level with mine.

Benidorm, a Spanish town along the Mediterranean Sea, has become a vacation hot spot, but at the time of Ted and Sylvia's honeymoon it was still a quaint seaside town.

In-Laws in Brontë Country

Elinor Klein, one of Sylvia's friends from Smith
Late August 1956

Heptonstall rolls, English countryside
cobwebbed by precise fences and little
houses huddled at hill peaks
like question marks. Ted hails from here.

Ted and Sylvia host well, but something
in the country air alters her, ignites
her outsider feelings. Sylvia raves
about the fat happy pigs, says her marriage

is like those contented hogs rolling
in the trough. Ted storytells of country
madness, the farmer who murders
all he owns and loves.

We visit a country witch,
but she reads the changing winds
of my life like an almanac,
not a crystal ball.

We traverse Wuthering Heights,
Sylvia sketches its glum remains.
We lose ourselves in the moor,
no end to the soft earth, no end to the fog.

Ted helps Sylvia fuse language with the land.
She trails him like a sheepdog,
picks up whatever he drops
or desires with her canine teeth.

She rubs her nose against his cheek,
and they do resemble contented pigs,
rooting around their mucky heaven
of stewed rabbit and Yeats.

This is not the Sylvia
I remember, that solo star,
that media darling. This Sylvia
is a sidekick, wife of the male lead.

Wuthering Heights (1847), Emily Brontë's only novel, is a story of doomed love and revenge and is considered among the masterpieces of English literature. Emily Brontë (1818–1848) was born in Thorton, Yorkshire, the moorland setting of *Wuthering Heights* visited by Ted, Sylvia, and Elinor Klein.

Boundless

Ted Hughes
Fall 1956

Her adoration
astonishes me.
Whether I merit it or not,
I don't know.

She leaps,
full throttle,
into this,
can't be stopped.

She needs me.
I umbrella her rain.
Shelter her
from pain.

I could devour her
but she has formed
this "We"
I live inside,

a clean house
where my muse settles,
where we gorge literature
and write well.

My poetry, my wife,
and I'm content,
that roly-poly hound,
bone clenched between my teeth.

According to his friend Michael Boddy, Ted was quite experienced with women and willingly offered dating advice. The night Ted met Sylvia, his girlfriend, Shirley, accompanied him to the *St. Botolph* party. He had been serious enough with Shirley to introduce her to his parents, but the relationship fell apart after he met Sylvia. Shirley, by most accounts, was the opposite of Sylvia—very English, very reserved.

Secretary

Aurelia Plath
      Fall 1956

I tried to school her in shorthand
that dreadful summer of 1953
when my Sivvy slipped beneath the surface
of language and breath.

Now she types and agents for him,
follows my footsteps in directions
I did not wish for her.
She manages the business of his writing,

but these efforts go underappreciated.
She feels refracted elation
when his work is accepted
as though *his* publishing, *his* poems were hers.

She sees Ted
as the larger talent
and herself as the vessel,
cargoing his work to the world.

How does a mother teach a daughter
to prize herself, not stand behind
the curtain of her man?
I have been a poor role model.

Sivvy must know
she is the star, no less bright
and necessary to the sky
than her husband.

She writes less, feels clogged
as a kitchen disposal.
She asks me for recipes,
not constructive literary criticism.

He may smother her.
His pillow of need
hangs softly over her head.
I fear he may cut off her breath.

During the fall of 1956 Sylvia was still attending Cambridge full-time and living
at Newnham Hall. She submitted not only Ted's work, but also her own. Sylvia
also found time to write fiction, poetry, and correspondence. Ted's poems appeared
in *The Nation, Poetry,* and *The Atlantic,* and he was reading his work regularly on
the BBC. While Sylvia was living apart from Ted, a lot of her work was being accepted and published as well. In this poem, Aurelia's fears are conveyed more as a
prediction of what lay ahead when Sylvia and Ted moved in together.

Secret

Professor Dorothea Krook, Sylvia's mentor and supervisor
in philosophy at Cambridge University
December 1956

Sylvia frantics, her breath short.
Words jet from her mouth.

She seeks advice. I tell her
to quell her anger over Cambridge rules,

plead love and passion, and come clean
about her unauthorized marriage to Ted.

I advise her to prostrate herself
before her tutor, strike a deal.

Sure enough, Sylvia is granted approval,
does not lose her scholarship, can live with Ted.

Her pride soars like a fire-stoked balloon.
She is the only married undergraduate.

She slips around Cambridge's stodgy policy
like a royal spy. Happiness flushes her skin.

I feel the heat of it when she enters my office.
I do wonder, like my fellow faculty,

whether Sylvia has chosen well for herself,
that maverick man, uncouth in culture and clothing.

•   Ted is rumored to annihilate—will he fuel
Sylvia or snuff her out? Marriage can box

an ambitious girl like Sylvia. She is more
than just a Mrs. Ted Hughes.

She cannot deny her largeness,
or madness may ensue.

Edward Butscher's *Sylvia Plath: Method and Madness* provides further insight into
this event, as does Dorothea Krook's unpublished memoir, housed at Smith College in the Edward Butscher Collection of Plath materials.

Complaints

Ted Hughes
        Winter 1957

Sylvia skulks about the flat,
cloaked in heavy sweater,
says the cold eats her bones.

She scours the floors,
but can't clean away the scum.
She can warm the bath

to only just above room temperature.
She rarely washes her hair
as it can't dry in this English rain and gloom.

She crouches soggy before the coal fire.
Her teeth chatter like cracking ice.
She grays, even amidst the robin's egg

blue walls of our first flat. Her numb
limbs pale against the bright davenport,
the streaming yellow light.

She needs sun to cheer,
needs space to breathe.
Sylvia, little princess of lament,

misses central heating, frozen food, refrigerators,
stoves that heat, new pipes, carpet sweepers.
Her list rolls farther than the horizon.

But when she calls our English literature
the academic's graveyard, I agree,
what prevails in London is dead poetry.

We will sail for America when the tulips bloom.

Ted chronicled his experiences of Sylvia in his poetry. He did not give interviews about Sylvia after she died until he brought out his collection *Birthday Letters* in 1998, a bestselling book of poems about his relationship with Sylvia.

Their Flat Creaks and Cries, "Money, Money"

Aurelia Plath
> *Winter 1957*

There is never enough.
Even on my small income I still have more.

I send them on holiday, deny myself
the tartan wool coat from the Sears catalogue,

make do with my old thrice pocket stitched
camel one, so that Sivvy can sun and write.

If only I had a son-in-law who provided,
steady as a plow horse, so their home held heat,

bread, and meat on the table. Sylvia writes
that Ted secured a job reading for the BBC

as though I should be jumping in my britches.
He radios Yeats's words and his own over the wires.

His audience expands. Sylvia posits that all
will soon be lovely, that success knocks

on their front door. But when I inquire
as to the frequency of these radio casts,

Sivvy admits the work is intermittent
as London sun, not to be relied upon,

a tiny windfall here and there, not security, nothing that will accrue in a bank account.

From Sylvia's November 21, 1956, letter to her mother (found in *Letters Home: Correspondence 1950–1963*):

". . . it has been a difficult time for both of us with no money coming in and the double expenses of Newnham and the new flat . . ."

". . . Thanks for the money; we'll have a good picture taken this vacation, you may be sure . . ."

At this time, Ted and Sylvia often used a Ouija board to try to pick winning lottery numbers. From her letter to Aurelia dated February 8, 1957:

"I do wish we could win the pools. Pan (our Ouija imp) . . . tells us more and more accurately. . . . If we won, we would deposit the money and live off the interest and write when and wherever we wanted and not get desperate about jobs."

Brute

Ted Hughes
    February 1957, Sylvia's last year at Cambridge

Sylvia mythologizes me
to the little Cambridge lasses
swirling at her feet.

I am a David, a lone rebel
fighting the English literary elite,
slaying monsters with my words.

Syl tells and retells how I drank
from a broken wine bottle when
no corkscrew could be found.

She crowns me as rugged and unruly,
a man's man brooding about
with my buddy Lucas Myers—

unsavory among the intellectuals,
carving my poems in wood,
inking them in boar's blood.

When I win the Poetry Center Award,
learn that Harper & Row will publish
my first book, *The Hawk in the Rain,*

in America and Faber's will bring it out
in Britain, Sylvia cannot be contained.
Rabid, frothing at the mouth, she announces

these successes as though we have
given birth to a son, a legacy.
I curl under my desk, exhausted

by her enthuse. I try to sit up straight
in my chair like the tower
of a man she constructs.

The Hawk in the Rain received plentiful and positive reviews. For example, according to Paul Alexander in Rough Magic:
"Library Journal contended that Hughes's poems had a 'striking field of vision'; [and] The New Statesman called Hughes a 'clearly remarkable poet.' "

The Wrong Man

Professor Mary Ellen Chase, one of Sylvia's teachers
and mentors at Smith
Spring 1957

I believe she has made a mistake,
married off her brain
to a brute.

Blessed with scholarship,
Sylvia doesn't need a man.
Still I recommend her to teach at Smith.

Perhaps distance from Britain
will help Sylvia
see Ted more clearly.

His crumpled shirt,
his sly smirk,
how he weights her down.

In January 1957 Mary Ellen Chase happened to be in Cambridge and met with Sylvia for coffee. Mary Ellen wrote a letter that basically secured Sylvia a teaching position at Smith. Chase did not meet Ted at this time but learned of his negative character traits from his former instructors. Both Paul Alexander's *Rough Magic* and Edward Butscher's *Sylvia Plath: Method and Madness* detail Mary Ellen Chase's reaction to Sylvia's marriage.

Boat to America

Imagining Sylvia Plath
In the style of "Mayflower"
June 1957

She boards the ship with no more than the clothes
In her trunk, his manuscripts, her bread pan.
She sucks in sea brine, brushes off Britain
Like dust on her sandals. She points her nose
Toward America, toward teaching. The woes
Of bitter cold, of student life be gone.
She is ocean. She'll provide. She will man
The home boat. He'll write. She'll keep them afloat.

Like pilgrims they travel into the new.
She sees herself happy. She'll slow her pace.
She'll be with her mother, her Ruth, her roots.
Her husband beside her, she'll find her place.
They'll have enough money, not just make do.
A bright shining future, a smiling face.

The poem "Mayflower" can be found in *The Collected Poems*. The sonnet is about the choice of the pilgrims to go to America and asserts that beauty is the best when, like a branch, it is hardy.

Professor Plath

Rosalie Horn, one of Sylvia's students at Smith
1957–1958

Hubbub buzzes about Sylvia,
bees draw around her honeycomb,
suckle from the star student
turned teacher, the royal sporting British attire.

Many of the girls in freshman English
took her course for the celebrity.
But Professor Plath shocks, outdoes
herself. They spotlight her blond curls

and she radiates. I have never had a teacher
in such a love affair with literature,
her brain an encyclopedia. She never fails
to answer our questions.

Even with a bad bout of flu I drag
my red nose to class. She talks typewriter
fast. I struggle to write it all down,
but when I look at my notes later, I am amazed.

I have been in the presence of genius.
I cry the last day of the semester.
I doubt I will ever again have a teacher
like Sylvia Plath.

Sylvia taught three freshman English classes, five days a week. She taught at Smith only one year. The college would have liked her to stay on, but teaching was too consuming and Sylvia was not able to both write and teach.

Sylvia and her Smith College roommate, Marcia Brown, 1951.

Sylvia and Joan Cantor on the beach in Cape Cod, 1952.

Sylvia at a Smith College dance, 1954.

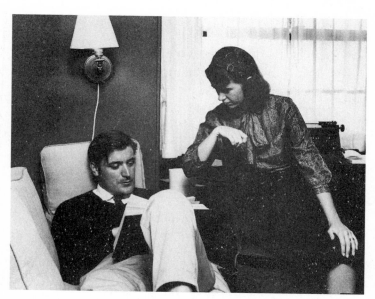

Sylvia and Ted in Boston, 1958. She was teaching at Smith College.

Massachusetts General Hospital

Myron "Mike" Lotz, an old boyfriend
        Sylvia reconnected with while back in the United States
        Fall 1958

I rub my eyes.
Behind a small table role-playing
as a desk, I imagine I see Sylvia,
a few years older, her blond hair
dulled into wheat.

Long resident hours wear heavy
as iron—this is not the first ghost
of my past I envisioned
traipsing down the hall.
I need some serious sleep.

Sylvia hollers, "Mike."
She tells me she's a secretary
in the psychiatric department, that she
finished her graduate work at Cambridge
and returned to the States, taught at Smith.
She tells me that she's married.

At her apartment I fill my wineglass
a few too many times. Her husband
is kind. A lovely English armoire, he seems
inanimate. I can't imagine him dancing
jigs around the room.

He is both rugged and elevated.
Ted hints to me that Sylvia is a handful
of nails, that he prefers a simple woman
like my escort tonight. I don't know
how to respond. I finish off my cabernet,
chatter on about nothing.

Ted was generally welcomed by all of Sylvia's friends, and upon initial meeting most found him charming and full of good humor, though to some he seemed condescending and aloof. Olive Higgins Prouty fell immediately under Ted's spell and wanted to put him on television. Marcia Brown Plummer at first thought Ted somewhat cold and distant, but came to feel that he was just shy. She eventually warmed to his charisma and skills as a raconteur. Later, her opinion of him altered as she witnessed Ted scold and humiliate Sylvia.

Robert Lowell's Poetry Class

Anne Sexton, poet, student of Lowell's, friend to Sylvia
Fall 1958–spring 1959

Sylvia stretches her skin
to fit someone else's bones—
her poems not yet her own.

George Starbuck, Syl, and I,
trinity of the master poet's class,
drink martinis, chow potato chips

at the Ritz, until slightly blitzed.
Drinks making us more real,
we talk suicide until laughter

tears from our eyes.
Then we bunch into my car
for the Waldorf Cafeteria's

seventy-cent dinner,
none of us having a better
or demanding home life to return to.

I implore Sylvia to push herself,
pluck the drum of her heart
until it bleeds. Sometimes I think

Lowell praises Sylvia too much,
or maybe he just sees something
in her language that I cannot.

Robert Lowell taught a seminar at Boston University that Sylvia attended along with fellow poets Anne Sexton and George Starbuck. Lowell introduced Sylvia to confessionalism, a kind of poetry defined by placing the literal Self at the center of the poem.

Robert Lowell (March 1, 1917–September 12, 1977), sometimes considered the father of confessional poetry, won the Pulitzer Prize for poetry in 1947 and 1974, and the National Book Award for poetry in 1960. He was hospitalized approximately twenty times for acute mania, which was treated with electroshock therapy.

Anne Sexton was an avowed confessional poet and helped to develop its precepts; critical acclaim for *To Bedlam and Part Way Back*, her first book, established her as a poet who wrote from experience. Sexton suffered from depression and had mental breakdowns and suicidal bouts. In the late fifties she began writing poetry as therapy and was soon "discovered" by the literary world for her unapologetically autobiographical poems. The recipient of many awards and grants, she won the Pulitzer Prize in 1966 for *Live or Die*. In 1974 she committed suicide by asphyxiation.

Anne Sexton said in her memoirs about her experience with Sylvia during the time of Lowell's class that she had ". . . heard since that Sylvia was determined from childhood to be great, a great writer at the least of it. I tell you, at the time I did not notice this in her. Something told me to bet on her but I never asked it why. I was too determined to bet on myself to actually notice where she was headed in her work. Lowell said, at the time, that he liked her work and that he felt her poems got right to the point. I didn't agree . . . I told Lowell that I felt she dodged the point and did so perhaps because of her preoccupation with form. Form was important for Sylvia . . . [but she] hadn't then found a form that belonged to her. Those early poems were all in a cage (and not even her own cage at that)."

Afraid

Dr. Beuscher, Sylvia's psychiatrist
1959

I see Sylvia every week,
my price adjusted to fit her budget.

She's not a little girl, never was.
She's a married woman afraid

of being a wife, afraid of sterility,
afraid to disappoint Ted, afraid

that she's lost her talent to domesticity,
afraid to admit that she did wish

her father dead, and afraid to tell
her mother she suffocates Sylvia

like a bee encased in glass,
no breathing holes. Oh, Sylvia buzzes

and flutters the jar, never ceasing.
She bangs her antennae

against thick glass until she falls, stunned.
Now she flees, afraid

to do the hard work of America.
Politics in her pocket, excuses

long as the dictionary, she runs
back to Britain. And I am afraid for her.

I love her like my own.
I cross lines and tell her this.

She eyes me, determined, says,
"Don't worry, Dr. Ruth. I will be fine."

In a 1998 interview with Karen Maroda, Dr. Beuscher said that she was not ambivalent about seeing Sylvia in 1959, that she "enjoyed seeing her," and she reluctantly admitted to Maroda that she loved Sylvia. Ruth did not encourage Sylvia to talk about Sylvia's feelings toward her (in standard psychoanalytic treatment the patient forms an attachment with the analyst and transfers feelings onto her); instead, she focused on Sylvia's feelings about her mother, Ted, and other important people in her life.

Maroda's interview with Ruth appeared as part of an article on www.salon.com on November 29, 2004.

Her Father's Grave

Imagining Sylvia Plath
In the style of "The Colossus"
1959

She dreams she delivered
The head, severed,
Blood-spattered between her legs.
Stillborn, skull eyes shocked
Into recognition.

She finds herself
Twenty years too late, unwell,
In a yard of the dead sleeping
Head to head. She teeters on Azalea Path,
Dusts off the black stone of Otto Plath.

She searches for the shovel,
Wants to dig Daddy up, cradle
Her father's skull, but the March ground
Remains hard. She thinks if she can look
Into his eyes, she might lose the dust from her own.

She dreams nightly now
Of unborn babies and unborn poems.
Stunted fetal fragments
That she loses like blood
Between her legs.

She thinks birth
Will save her.
Dr. Beuscher warns,
"After babies
The depression will be worse."

"The Colossus" is the title poem from Sylvia's first collection of poetry, *The Colossus and Other Poems*. "The Colossus" is a myth-making poem about her father in which Sylvia sees him as a titanic but lifeless statue, a powerful force and relationship in her life that she does not understand.

Her Poetry

Ted Hughes
Summer 1959

We drive this country,
camp and swim and breathe
the Midwest in,
drive sunrise to sunset
until thick in Bear Country
and redwoods we stop.

Sylvia can find no poetry
in this land, only superstitions
and tales of unhappy marriages.
I find lines in ringed trunks,
fallen pine needles,
low clouded sky.

She swells now with our first child,
no doctor's confirmation required,
we know the baby thrives.
Maybe it feeds on her words, her lyricism,
absorbs nutrients of language,
leaves little for the mother.

I tell Syl to relax,
soak in this birth, let her poems
gestate. They will be born.
Sylvia should write
her woman's rag stories
and lie content in the cool noon sun.

We stay at Yaddo, the writers' colony,
this fall. She will be released there,
I predict it. What this baby will do
to her writing, I can't predict.
Will the newborn's cries offer her melody,
or will they cause her to go deaf?

Chronicled in Sylvia's short story "The Fifty-ninth Bear," Bear Country refers to Devil's Cauldron in Yellowstone National Park.

Ted initially did not want to have any children. He did not want the burden of having to financially support children or to lose his freedom to explore the world. But Sylvia had her heart set on having a baby, and Ted wanted to make her happy. During this cross-country trip Ted was finishing up *Lupercal*, his second book of poetry, which was scheduled to be released by Faber and Faber the following spring.

Autumn

Aurelia Plath
Autumn 1959

My baby and unborn grandbaby
will sail away.

Sylvia cannot live in America's
summer. She must leave,

follow the cold. In the fall,
in the earth's dying, she finds creation.

I knead the dough of my bread,
knuckles deep in flour, and wish

that birth was her mantra. But Sivvy
has been a child of the graveyard,

haunted by ghosts, since the day
Otto died. I can't reach far enough

into the ground to pull her back
and hold her here.

Ted had wanted to return to England since the beginning of 1959. Sylvia finally agreed in May 1959 that they would move back that fall. She did not like living in Boston and was struggling to have any of her work published. Sylvia requested, as part of the deal, that Ted buy her an icebox and that they find a good dentist.

Sister-in-Law

Olwyn Hughes, Ted's sister
December 1959

They return,
December with us in Yorkshire.

Ted's weary, his face
softened by American soaps

and all the trinkets designed
so one never dirties one's hands.

The mind freezes overseas,
harsher than our British

blustering gales, their
manufactured comfort.

I miss my brother, try to sneak
time to speak with him alone,

but Sylvia creeps around every corner,
must add words to our sentences,

her dull Pollyanna enough
to make one vomit sugarcane.

How he chose such a wife,
I'll never comprehend.

A pretty face, a belly swollen
with child.

Ted deserves better, deserves
royalty. I will never lower myself

for a man any less grand than my brother.
Why did he choose someone so beneath me?

Olwyn's correspondence with Sylvia and the interviews she has given for biographies of Sylvia record her view of her sister-in-law. Olwyn worked in Paris, at various times, as a secretary for both the North Atlantic Treaty Organization and a theatrical agency. She never married.

Homemaker

Marcia Brown Plummer,
Sylvia's best friend in America
February 1960

A flat on Chalcot Square
where she scrubs and retiles
and paints and styles
to furnish and polish
while builders demolish
the apartments surrounding her—
it's astounding that Sylvia
can call such a place home.

Birth heavy and in-lawed-out,
Sylvia builds her nest to assuage her doubts.
No extra bedroom for the baby,
Freud and Spock would call her crazy
to raise a family in such close quarters.
But this was all they could afford.
And she loves her little "house,"
remains enchanted with her spouse.
I miss her like gloves
on a frostbite day. I send her
my love from an ocean away.

Sylvia and Marcia corresponded throughout Sylvia's life.

Poetry First

Ted Hughes
         March 1960

Baby about to come,
my book *Lupercal* praised,
I'm pushed into the posh lounge

of esteemed British poets—
Eliot, Spender, and the like.
My wife also will see her
first book born in print.

Britain adores us,
gathers us under smoky wings
so poetry comes
before labor pains.

We are artists first,
our children will be
second works.

Ted Hughes's book *Lupercal* received excellent reviews and transformed Ted into a major figure in British poetry. It allowed Ted and Sylvia introduction into London's literary set.

The Birth of Frieda Rebecca

Sister Mardi, Sylvia's first midwife
April 1, 1960

I leap to my bicycle,
cross myself that Mrs. Hughes
has only begun pre-labor,
but she pains severe,
her forehead crinkles,
her hands clenching
her husband's wrist like a vise.

Mrs. Hughes pleads through
her brow-sweat for medicine,
but the baby is too far along.
Mr. Hughes rubs her back
and the baby arrives quickly,
slides out of its mother
without agony, with only a bitty cry.

I tell Mrs. Hughes what fortune
smiles in her home, only
four and a half hours of labor.
She must have birthed many children
in a previous life. I scrub the baby
in a Pyrex bowl, swaddle her
in the cradle beside her parents' bed.

I advise Mrs. Hughes to rest,
keep her feet under cover, sleep
like the deceased, but I see devil
in her eye, she will disobey.
This birth was too easy.
Restless as a kitten, Mrs. Hughes must
leap about, bat at her balls of string.

Frieda Rebecca Hughes was born April 1, 1960, in London at home in the flat at
Chalcot Square. In England in 1960, the National Health Service provided free
prenatal care and midwife services for home delivery and the first fourteen days of
a baby's life.

Baby Girl

Imagining Sylvia Plath
In the style of "Morning Song"
April 1960

I have waited for you, your heartbeat
Inside me like the clock's ticking
Second hand. I still feel your pulse when I sleep.

You are your father's daughter, just like I was.
He loves you like a fine sentence.
He feeds you and you feed him.

I do not own you, my little one,
But I hope to rent space in your heart, hold tight
Your small hands that clench and mimic my own.

I write between bottles and nappies
And the breakfast table. I type while your daddy
Wheels you through the first blooms of spring.

Send me lines deeper than my tired, wrinkled brow.
Teach me innocence and beginning
And I will sing you my music, rhythm you to sleep.

A little starling, you yawp for my drizzle of milk.
I fill you, helium you into the sky like a pink balloon
So that you soar, our family a trinity of heaven, sun, and song.

"Morning Song" is the first poem in *Ariel*. Sylvia wanted to begin the collection with the word "love." "Morning Song" opens "Love set you going like a fat gold watch." Written on February 19, 1961, the poem is about her daughter, Frieda Rebecca. In a letter, Sylvia wrote that the "whole experience of birth and baby seem(s) much deeper, much closer to the bone, than love and marriage."

Mr. and Mrs. Ted Hughes

A. Alvarez, poetry editor of the Observer,
later became one of Ted's drinking buddies
Summer 1960

Two tall people and baby crammed
into a flat so small you must maneuver it
sideways. Yet the Hughes' home burbles
with productivity, happiness.

I so loved Ted Hughes' second book,
Lupercal, that I determined to befriend the man.
We walk our children through the zoo
and plan to do a BBC program together.

Mrs. Hughes seemed nice upon first meeting,
offered me cherry torte and tea,
a pinafored mother,
her home clean and warm.

When she shakes my hand and thanks me
for publishing her poem, I nearly choke
on my chamomile tea. She laughs awkwardly,
"I'm Sylvia Plath."

A year before their meeting, Alvarez had accepted Sylvia's poem "Night Shift." A lot of Sylvia's poems were being published in 1960. In June her poems appeared in the *Critical Quarterly,* the *London Magazine,* and the *Partisan Review.* In July her verses were published in *Harper's* and the *Atlantic Monthly.* In August the *New Yorker* printed her poem "The Net-Menders." Ironically, she wasn't able to create any new poetry during this period.

Alvarez is best known for his 1972 book *The Savage God: A Study of Suicide,* which gained added resonance from his friendship with Sylvia Plath and discusses her suicide.

Appendectomy

Ted Hughes
February–March 1961

Sylvia loses another part
of herself, first the miscarriage
and now an organ—two
large holes in her center.

Frieda cries, tosses her potatoes
on the floor; and I can't manage
to wash a single dish.
How does Sylvia do this and write?

The hospital is peace to her.
She's free within the nurse-
watched ward, white and cleaner
white—shoes, hats, bedsheets.

Sylvia stares at the tulips
sent courtesy of her mentor,
the renowned poet Ted Roethke.
She writes reclined in bed.

The quiet, still, germy air
allows her to think.
She breathes by tubes,
but her mind is unbound.

She writes and writes and writes and writes . . .

Sylvia miscarried on February 2, 1961, the day after she and Ted had attended a party for Theodore Roethke, an acclaimed American poet. Sylvia was depressed, but turned out seven poems in the days following her miscarriage, including "Parliament Hill Fields," "Morning Song," "Face Lift," and "Barren Woman." Frieda Rebecca Hughes was ten months old at the time. You can feel the push and pull of Sylvia's joy over Frieda and sadness about the miscarriage in some of these poems. Because of the miscarriage, her appendectomy was performed earlier than scheduled. During her recovery Sylvia wrote the poems "Tulips" and "I Am Vertical," among others. Sylvia's longer poem "Three Women: A Poem for Three Voices" was inspired by her hospital stay. All of the aforementioned poems can be found in *The Collected Poems*.

Theodore Roethke (1908–1963) was awarded the Pulitzer Prize for poetry in 1954 for his book *The Waking*.

BBC

Lucas Myers, Ted's closest friend
March 1961

They talk—
her chatterbox,
his fierce tongue and low sonar,
Britain's poet couple.

I lost part of Ted
when they married,
could not see gold
on Sylvia's page,

but he assured me,
she will become
stardust,
a voice remembered.

I'm shocked to learn
she included my work
in that anthology
of promising poets she edited.

I hope this does not
place me in her debt.
I flip on my radio,
hear the rebroadcast of Sylvia and Ted.

The BBC show that Ted and Sylvia were on was called *Two of a Kind*, a program
that featured interviews with married couples who worked in the same field. Sylvia
and Ted's show was titled "Poets in Partnership" and was taped on January 18,
1961, and aired March 19, 1961.

The Hughes' Plan to Buy a Home in Devon

Aurelia Plath
1961

I cash another CD
as though I have no future to save for,
nothing at home to repair,
to help them purchase a house,
two acres in the country,
a big thatched cottage,
a storybook manse.
Sylvia rhapsodizes, "Oh, the flowers,
Mother, the daffodils.
So bountiful we'll sell
cartloads of them.
We can grow carrots and cabbage,
be self-sufficient out there
and pay you back.
Someday, we'll return to you
all that we have borrowed."

I shake my head across the ocean.
A mother doesn't loan.
She gives.

From *Letters Home: Correspondence 1950–1963*:

In a letter to Warren dated July 30, 1961, Aurelia conveys excitement about Ted and Sylvia's new home, but admits:

"Both Edith [Ted's mother] and I are each loaning 500 pounds so they won't be snowed under by the terrible interest rate. . . . I was willing to take the whole mortgage at 3 percent, but Ted would not listen to it, and I admire his determination to be as independent as possible."

Ted and Sylvia bought Court Green for 3,600 pounds, what was roughly the equivalent of $10,000 at the time.

Christmas at Yorkshire, 1961

Elizabeth Compton, Sylvia's friend and neighbor in Devon

The other side of this
I know nothing about, but Sylvia
tensed as she unwove the tale,
her hands rock-rigid and her tongue
lashing rapid speed.

Sylvia had asked Olwyn, Ted's sister,
finally, why she hated her so.
And Olwyn unleashed among
the cranberries and fruitcake
that Sylvia was a spoiled interloper,
trying to usurp Olwyn's role
in the Hughes family.

Sylvia cried, banged her once-again-pregnant
body up the stairs, believing they
all hated her. She waited for Ted,
who had witnessed the row,
to ascend the stairs and comfort her.

Ted remained in his armchair,
read his book, played Switzerland,
did not want to enter the catfight.
Sylvia, eight months heavy with his child,
felt betrayed. She dashed from the house
in light overcoat, slippered feet,
and waded into the foggy moor.

She awaited her husband,
but again his outline did not appear
in the mist. Hours passed like weeks,
the ground wet. Frigid air knocked
her over. She laid down in the fern grass,
drowsy as though drugged, clutched
her belly, and shut her eyes.

Ted, candlestick in hand,
found her halfway up the moor,
a Catherine turning blue as a ghost.
He carried her home.

Olwyn left
the next morning for Paris
before Sylvia woke,
before the family
finished their coffee.

Ted and Sylvia and Frieda returned
to their home at Court Green.

Sylvia breathes over her tea,
fills the pot, smells her leaves.
She examines the bottom
of her cup, says, "Things
will never be the same,"
as she crafts a thank-you
letter to Ted's parents.

I stir cream and honey
into my cup, almost tell Sylvia
that in-laws are boiling pots
on everyone's stove
and need to be handled carefully,
but I don't want to stick
my two farthings in a bank
I really know nothing about.

Sylvia chronicled her difficulties with her husband in her journals and then later
in letters she wrote to Aurelia and others.

Son

Ted Hughes
January 1962

Nick jumped into the world
cold in Nurse Davies's hands,
shriveled skull with a thatch
of dark fuzz. He fusses little.

Sylvia says he's quiet
like his father. I guess we've
become that station-wagon family
they advertise on the American tube.

Sylvia claims she feels poetry in childbirth.
I love my daughter, but she and her brother
are too little to hold my pen,
let alone guide it into words.

Nicholas Farrar Hughes was born January 17, 1962, at the Hughes' home, Court Green, in Devon.

Woman of the House

Sylvia Crawford, a Devon neighbor,
mother of three daughters
Winter 1962

I don't know how she does it
(except that she hires both a nanny and a maid,
unusual for around here,
very upper crust and city-folkish).
I don't know how she manages
that manor with needlepoint precision
and writes her poems too
(of course, her husband
minds the children mornings
so she can lock herself up in her study,
a sign on her door that says
"Leave Me Alone").

We talk about nappies and prams,
what temperature to heat bottles,
groan together over our exhaustion
and our babies' teething tantrums.
Sylvia strains to maintain interest
in us and our baby talk.
She's not like my other friends,
an exiled queen on her little estate.
I don't know how she gets by,
she is so singular, so unusual, so alone.

Court Green, the Hughes' home, was a large cottage located at the summit of the town of Croton. Croton was more cement-gray and plain than the lush and green Devon, but the church across the street dated from the twelfth century, and Sylvia loved living among the daily evidence of Croton's medieval history. Sylvia was considered a "lady of the house," as the town still kept to class distinctions at that time. However, Sylvia's friendly American ways broke down those boundaries and she was well liked by most in the village. Still, she and Ted were artists first and therefore always considered outsiders.

Routine

Aurelia Plath
Winter 1962

Recovered from surgery,
childbirth, and her usual
winter maladies, Sylvia
reinstates a schedule.

Nick sleeps through the night,
which allows her to write mornings.
I call this dedication,
my daughter claims it's survival.

Without poetry she would crumble
like a dried-out lemon cake,
stale and inedible. She talks
bright, but something in her has hardened.

I think this life of two children,
two literary careers, multiple gardens,
and too many rooms to dust
must exhaust her weak constitution.

On the surface Sivvy looks the same,
long, swept-up hair, red smile,
poems published every month.
She stands beside her husband,

stalwart, like the day they married,
but I know something
in the photo she mailed me
is off.

Aurelia expressed some of her concerns about Sylvia's life directly to Sylvia in letters. In the introduction to *Letters Home: Correspondence 1950–1963*, Aurelia illuminates retrospectively her concerns about Sylvia's marriage in 1962.

Elm

*Ruth Fainlight, poet, London friend of Sylvia and Ted's
May 1962*

We drink it black,
mud-thick, steam misting
over our cups.

I see something bitter
as coffee in Sylvia's eyes,
wish that London were not so far
from Devon. Sylvia pines
so for a friend who is her equal.

We read each other our latest
poems, and I can't breathe
when she finishes "Elm."
I shiver. Her words like porcupine
quills prick my skin. They haunt
and possess me like a shadow.

I touch her hand, so cold
the coffee cup can't warm it.
She unravels a bit, her hemline
hangs low in back and I fear
she might lose that rhythm that kills, that kills.
And that might kill her.

Ruth Fainlight married Alan Sillitoe, the novelist best known for his book *The Loneliness of the Long-Distance Runner*. Sillitoe had won the Hawthornden Prize the year before it was awarded to Ted Hughes, and the couples met as a result. Sylvia and Ruth became close, and Sylvia expressed in letters how much she missed London and city life. In May 1962, Ruth and Sylvia had both recently given birth to sons, another link that brought them closer together.

Ruth Fainlight is an award-winning author who has published thirteen collections of poems in England and the United States, as well as two volumes of short stories.

Her Fan

A. Alvarez, poetry editor of the Observer,
    one of Ted's drinking buddies
    May 1962

I read her first collection, *The Colossus*.
Unlike most critics, I like it.
I find her work unfeminine.
She, like her husband, writes good poetry.

I do, however, wish she'd settle on her own style.
She shies from her true voice. Her poetry withholds
like she does—Sylvia presents as competent,
kind, excellent with her children,
a well-crafted housewife, but like a photo
out of someone else's magazine.

Her poetry too executes beautifully,
flawless rhythms, but it smacks of others—
Roethke, Wallace Stevens. And she stands
in the shadow of her own Ted Hughes.
There is more to her, bubbling quietly on the stove,
ready to scream, if only she'll release it.

Female poets of note who were Sylvia's contemporaries and whose work endures
today include Adrienne Rich, Anne Sexton, Stevie Smith, and Maxine Kumin.

Sylvia

Assia Wevill, a married woman who will become
Ted's mistress
May 1962

She is poetry,
that mother of language,
and I am a Gypsy,
wandering, thieving what I fancy.

She is cunning
like an old watchdog,
she sees the scene
without being present.
I am experienced.
I have thrown my nightgown
over more than one man's head.

She snarls,
tries to make me squirm,
and I pity her,
trapped in this life
of two kids and a fading husband,
clutching her notebooks
as though they are friends.

She bakes. She gardens.
She follows her routine.
I flit freely among her flower beds
and he chases me, tired
of Sylvia dragging
him along like a can tied
to a bumper.

He cuts her fraying rope,
rolls down the hill
and into my bed.

Assia and her husband, David, leased the Hughes' London flat. Ted and Assia began their extramarital relationship in the summer of 1962.

Losing

Imagining Sylvia Plath
        In the style of "Event"
        Summer 1962

The night is indigo and she is gray.
He cannot see her among the shadows.
There was a time she was a rabbit he longed to snare.

Now her simmering pot grows cold,
Charcoal crusted. She lifts the lid, there's nothing inside.
The babies waddle the floorboards blind.

The temperature drops. She pulls the blanket over their
    heads.
Oh, he is absent as November blossom.
He tends nothing but his own words.

He says it's her fault there's no harvest this year.
He says it with his silent hand.
He won't look at her face long enough to slap her.

She waves the white flag of her soul, her shirt
Damp on the line. She knows the woman of night
And silk stockings bewitches with her musk perfume.

She smells it on him, blood and London and cheer.
All she cooks up is a pot of gloom.
She has no arm to hold out anymore. Gangrene

Settles in. She is without a limb.
In her dreams she still runs after Daddy,
That hair shirt ghost who never looks back.

She screams without sound. She has been muted out.

Plath's poem "Event," about a relationship that has been dismembered, can be found in *The Collected Poems*.

Sylvia's Book Doesn't Sell

Knopf editorial assistant
Summer 1962

Predictions like weather reports,
we thought the Plath collection
would sell like summer sun,

but the book languishes, sinks
in a gray rain. I can't explain
why. The buzz is that Sylvia

has not the talent, has not
the emotional depth. Pity
that her language embraces

one like a proud father. Pity
that this father expects so much of her,
is not a parent of love
but of the balance sheet.

Knopf published *The Colossus and Other Poems* in America on May 14, 1962.

A Letter to the Successful Poet

Mother of Keith Douglas, a little-known English poet
who died in World War II at the age of twenty-four
June 1962

Dear Master Hughes,
I wish to thank you
heartily for my son,
who cannot.
I have read all your books,
your selected works
penned so young,
you are only thirty-one,
and I feel you've just become
my hero.
I want you to know
that Keith is honored by you.
I hope you continue
to shine starlight
on other little-known men,
the work of their pens,
because today success seems dependent
on being recommended
by great writers like you.
So thank you. Thank you. Thank you.

From Paul Alexander's *Rough Magic:* "Hughes wielded so much power that on his recommendation alone, a whole career could be made—or resurrected. . . . [I]n late May [1962] [he] broadcast a radio show on Keith Douglas, a British poet killed at the age of twenty-four in Normandy in World War II. On the basis of Hughes's single broadcast, Faber decided, provided that Hughes would write an introduction, to issue a 'selected' edition of Douglas's poems, much to the delight of Douglas's impoverished mother, who wrote Hughes to thank him."

New Affiliates

Charlie Pollard, Devon's best and foremost member
of the Beekeepers' Society
June 1962

Sylvia tends the hive well.
Her husband bumbles
and his back's full of stingers.

Sylvia transfers queens
from one hive to the next
so that a virgin bee ascends

the throne. The old one's
outgrown her little home
and moves on.

Sylvia's husband skips meetings,
absent as summer snow.
I marvel at how she grows

her garden and home alone
and still manages the bees,
cares for their honeycomb.

In a letter to her mother, Sylvia wrote that the local bee meeting was "attended by the rector, the midwife, and assorted beekeeping people from neighboring villages." In her journal entry of June 7, 1962, Sylvia describes the constituents of the Beekeepers' Society as "a group of miscellaneous Devonians . . . an assortment of shapeless men in brown speckled bulgy tweeds . . . [and] two women, one very large, tall, stout, in a glistening aqua-blue raincoat, the other cadaverous as a librarian in a dun raincoat."

June 1962

Aurelia Plath

1. The Perfect Home

I arrive at Court Green
welcomed by a room
of painted pink hearts and flowers
and a granddaughter who blurts,
"Hello, Granny," without provocation.

New Baby Nick bounces
smiling into my arms like we are old
friends. The manor, well kept
and lovely, groomed gardens
and flower beds, hand-painted furniture,
a lemon cake cooling on the counter.
But underneath the sweet scent
something bitter simmers,
trapped in the walls—
a festering mold black enough
to make one cough,
an odor rotten enough to stop breath.

Sivvy announces repeatedly
that happiness dances around her bed.
She has the perfect home, the perfect
children, the perfect husband.
But I believe she doth protest too heartily.
Still, I button my lip, dare not contradict
her, but the tension in the air's
thick and deadly as smog.

2. Loss of Faith

When Sylvia's neighbor Percy dies
of cancer, Sivvy crashes.
The strain on my daughter's shoulders
so great she cannot bear
loss or disruption.

Sivvy submits the final section
of her first novel to the foundation
supporting her work. She reveals
that she's nearly finished her
second novel, about a young American
girl in England who falls for a heroic man
and marries him. She intends to give
a first draft of the new book to Ted
as a birthday present.

She frets that the writing
on this novel stagnates lately.
Sylvia can't bring her pen
to the page. I fear she has lost faith
in her male protagonist.

Sylvia had never been to a funeral before she attended Percy Key's on June 29, 1962. An excerpt from her Journal 1962, Appendix 15 found in *The Journals of Sylvia Plath: 1950–1962*, illustrates some of her reactions:

". . . Rose [Percy's wife] rapt and beautiful and frozen, the Catholic dropping a handful of earth which clattered. A great impulse welled in me to cast earth also, but it seemed as if it might be indecent, hurrying Percy into oblivion. We left the open grave. An unfinished feeling. Is he to be left there uncovered, all alone?"

As to Sylvia's novel:

The central events of Sylvia's early life, particularly those of the summer and fall of 1953, when she was a guest editor for *Mademoiselle*, attempted suicide, and underwent hospitalization, form the basis of her only novel, *The Bell Jar*. Sometimes referred to as a confessional novel, *The Bell Jar* is a fictional autobiography that Sylvia often called her "pot-boiler," as she did not consider it to be a "serious work." The novel follows Esther Greenwood, a sensitive young artist, as she questions the world around her, searches for identity, and descends into madness. It has become a widely read and seminal work.

Shopping in Exeter

Aurelia Plath
 July 9, 1962

Sylvia steers the Morris,
chipper as a baby bluebird,
proclaims that she has everything
in life she has ever wanted.

I nod and stare out the window,
green hills roll like waves
across the countryside.

We tire of shopping early,
decide to return to Court Green
after lunch. Sylvia hears the phone
blare when she enters her house.

She rushes to grab the receiver.
Ted tops the stairs, startled
by our presence, stares at the phone,

dashes toward it. He misses a step,
falls backward, and bumps down
each stair, a snowball gathering speed,
until he crashes onto the floor.

Sivvy picks up the phone
with a calm "Hello."
A pause the length of an epic poem

and she accuses the caller,
"I know who this is, Assia,
no need to disguise your voice."
Sylvia hands Ted the phone.

He swiftly rids himself of his lady
caller. Sivvy's anger inflates her
ten feet tall. She yanks the telephone

wire out of the wall. I back up,
my arms around Frieda, covering
her eyes from the scene in the hallway.
The house is so quiet you hear only the wind.

Sivvy bundles up Baby Nick,
bolts from the house, leaving
Frieda under my care.

Ted stands ten seconds
in the hallway watching Sylvia go
and I am left without words.
I want to exit, but my legs stick to the floor.

I wish he would vanish,
burst into oblivion
like a soap bubble.

Should I scold him like a child,
should I pretend that nothing's awry?
I fume that he has made me awkward
in my daughter's house.

I decide *not* to make him tea,
clutch my grandbaby to my chest
and back away from it all.

Sylvia and Ted had bought their Morris station wagon the previous summer
(1961). Aurelia visited Court Green from June 21 until August 4, 1962. After the
incident in the above poem, Aurelia stayed with Winifred Davies, Sylvia's midwife and friend, for the last few weeks of her trip. This vacation was the last time
Aurelia would see Sylvia alive. In the summer of 1962, Frieda was two and
Nicholas was six months old.

Sylvia Begins to Tell the Truth

Elizabeth Compton,
*   Sylvia's friend and neighbor in Devon*
*   July 1962*

Sylvia looks as though she's been hit
by a hailstorm.
Nick gurgles in his carry cot.
She speaks fast
and loud, no sun in her tone.

She can't feed Nick, her milk
has dried up, her milk
is gone. Nick will starve. She drops
the baby in the front hall,
shakes off her outer garments, gloves,
scarf, hat, overcoat
as she marches into the parlor.

She weeps, "Help me." Her eyes never
stop flowing tears.
Ted loves another woman, Assia.
Ted lies to her.
I grab her hand, don't know what to say,
don't know how to calm her.
She flinches at my touch. I stick my finger
in Nick's mouth
so at least the baby soothes, becomes quiet and calm.

I tell Sylvia she should stay the night
with us, then haul out
the guest linens, tuck Sylvia
into bed like a child.
She stares blankly, eyes swollen red,
her nose drips.
She says, "When you give someone
your whole heart
and he doesn't want it, you cannot
take it back.
It's gone forever."

Sylvia's quote at the end of this poem is from "Sylvia in Devon: 1962," written by Elizabeth (Compton) Sigmund in *Sylvia Plath: The Woman and the Work*, edited by Edward Butscher.

Burning: Summer of Bonfires

Imagining Sylvia Plath
In the style of "Poppies in July"
1962

She starts with the stack of wood he chopped,
Logs and planks piled high. Adds in a bit of kindling.

But the ingredient that makes the flames rise
Is words. Her papers and letters crinkle and pop,

Shrivel and ravel like withered blooms.
Each week she shovels in something new.

Slaughters the novel she etched of their love.
Destroys the stationery she posted across an ocean—

Her hope set sail, now ash. The fumes,
The smoke catch in her throat.

She burns his papers too, the typed manuscripts
She secretaried. She dances Rumpelstiltskin

Round the pyre of poetry, incants his name.
Maybe a new phoenix will rise from the flames,

From the cold, colorless char.

"Poppies in July" can be found in *Ariel* and is included in *The Collected Poems*. It was the second poem Sylvia wrote after Assia's phone call. The poem questions whether poppies, the flower and the opiate, do harm when they numb and dull. It is a poem of anger and resignation.

Pretense

Ted Hughes
> *August 15, 1962*

She burns my work
so I leave no papers in the house,
so I leave the house now,
return to Court Green weekends only.

See and tend the children weekends only
as my "home" is an infirmary,
a place of colds and flu.
I am not running away, I am running to.

Sylvia and I agree to play
happy couple for her patron,
Mrs. Prouty, force smiles
through an evening of dinner and theater.

But a night alone at the Connaught Hotel
with Sylvia's dagger eyes
and venom tongue pantomiming,
"Bad father, bad husband, bad man,"

no wonder I can't stand
to be in her presence.
She incinerates herself with anger,
cannot write knee-deep in spite.

When Sylvia asks for a legal separation
I am relieved.

Sylvia believed that Ted maintained a secret flat in London where he stayed during the week over the summer. However, most likely he stayed with his friend the renowned poet W. S. Merwin, and his wife, Dido, or on A. Alvarez's sofa. He confided in the Merwins, Alvarez, and obviously in Assia about the problems he had with Sylvia.

Child Support

Elizabeth Compton,
Sylvia's friend and neighbor in Devon
August 1962

Nick needs male tending.
Fatherless, he hides under
her skirt.

Sylvia rages hot as coal
though the weather chills. She says
she wishes Ted were dead.

It's easier for a child
to understand a father
underground. Not a runaway.

She scrubs his scent
from the sheets,
from the house.

She cashes his little checks—
the only thing
he gives his children now.

In August 1962 Ted was mostly living in London, though he spent weekends at Court Green, and when Sylvia fell ill with a terrible fever he returned to Devon to help with the children.

On August 25, 1962, John Malcolm Brinnin, Dylan Thomas's biographer, courted Ted about replacing him at the University of Connecticut the following year, but Ted turned the offer down. The unsettled matters in his personal life likely contributed to his decision.

Can a Vacation in Ireland Rescue Their Marriage?

Richard Murphy, Irish poet whom Sylvia awarded
first prize in the Guinness Awards
September 1962

A couple of warring cats—
Sylvia hisses and claws. Ted silent, sneaky,
lurks about the house.
They sleep in separate twin beds,
tell me, over pints,
too much about their marriage.

We ferry out to see Yeats's Coole Park.
Sylvia insists Ted etch his initials
next to Yeats's, but Ted's pants leg
catches on the spiked fence. We huff up
the tower's spiral staircase instead.

Sylvia tosses coins, throws back her arms
howling, sniffs up the spirit
of the master. Ted doesn't react
as though her behavior's abnormal.

They each pull me aside,
ask me to play marriage counselor.
He's seeing another woman.
She wants to separate.

I have been stuck
in the molasses of divorce before
and advise her, as a friend,
to make the break clean—

but Sylvia talks to herself,
desires me to simply play mirror,
nod when she nods, laugh when she chortles,
cry out the tears dried
in the corner of her eyes.

Ted plays Ouija while we sleep,
slips out the next day. She launches
excuses for his departure,
but they are so weak
a breeze knocks them down.

He abandons her again.

Under the table Sylvia brushes
my knee. I ask her to leave—
will not be scratched
by those claws,
will not have her dropping
dead birds at my feet.

Richard Murphy's epilogue "Years Later" to his poem "The Cleggan Disaster" won
first prize in the 1962 Guinness Awards. More information on Sylvia and Ted's
last-ditch vacation to Ireland can be found in Paul Alexander's biography *Rough
Magic*.

Disappear

Aurelia Plath
Autumn 1962

I feared this—
his black demeanor,
towering silence,
sporting the superior
threadbare jacket of the artist.
He doesn't even
phone to inquire
about the children.

Sylvia opens the wounds
she has hidden from me—
the deep lacerations in her back—
Ted neglects Nicholas,
Ted tells her he never wanted children.
Ted has left her,
and her alone darkens
like a cellar door
drawing closed.

Aurelia suggested that Sylvia move back home, but Sylvia refused. She could not face her mother after Aurelia had witnessed the dissolution of her marriage. Sylvia's mind-set is conveyed in her October 9, 1962, letter, published in *Letters Home: Correspondence 1950–1963*:

". . . America is out for me. I want to make my life in England. If I start running now, I will never stop. I shall hear of Ted all my life, of his success, his genius . . . I must make a life of my own as fast as I can . . ."

The Arrival of Poetry

Imagining Sylvia Plath
In the style of "The Arrival of the Bee Box"
October 1962

She wakes shaking, her coffee
Rattles its cup like a brass bell, her babies
Rattle their prams, but she cannot
Stop her pen writing.
Her words arrive, a box to be opened.

Pretty on the outside, blue-bowed
And wrapped in the crisp paper of autumn,
Her words resonate danger.
Her poems are like a box of apples,
Sour and tart in her mouth,
They predict a fall.

She feels like a medium.
She catches lines like a sieve.
She slices a vein and poetry flows,
Blood dark, blood dirty,
A river into Hades.

She blocks Ted out, the rake, her children's
Unfaithful father, invisible as the man who draws
The stage curtain, who ties up the show.
She doesn't need him
To tell her when to begin, when to end.

Poetry taps beat after beat
From her typewriter keys.
She studies the page, astonished
At her maniac poems, buzzing real as an ear.
She cannot send them back.

She cannot remember writing them down.
She can only remember the way
The words felt, honest as a morning moon.
And she is their creator,
Standing alone in her laurel crown.

She escapes this way.
Her early-morning pen
Breaks the kill hours, cleanses her in blood,
Burns the wrinkles from her face.
She radiates language.

She will not be shut up, will not be eclipsed.

October 1962, the month of Sylvia's thirtieth birthday, would prove to be Sylvia's most prolific month of writing poetry. Most of the poems in *Ariel* were written in this month, in the early mornings between three a.m. and dawn, when the children awoke. She called these hours "the kill hours." During the first week of October Sylvia wrote five poems she collectively called "Bees." They deal—if not overtly, then inadvertently—with her father. Otto had studied bees, was a beekeeper, and had authored *Bumblebees and Their Ways*.

All the Bitter Things

Ted Hughes
October 11, 1962

On the train I wish
I had swallowed my tongue,
that I had suffered laryngitis,
anything not to have said
all those horrible things to her.

But she witches me, her superior
mug of the bitch, her pointy finger,
she clings to blame like a mantra.
She never knew how nightmarish
living with her was.

All the years I spent jailed
in a narrow hallway, responding
to her thousand daily calls,
trying to scrawl my poems
between her spasms, her charcoal moods.

My hands form a noose,
I wanted to crack her neck
when she refused to give me
the remainder of her Saxton Grant.
Oh, the wicked part of my heart flared.

Assia and I think perhaps
Sylvia will kill herself;
David, Assia's husband,
attempted suicide when Assia left him,
and he was strong.

Boarding the train, Sylvia's judgment
eyes catch me and I say it—
I had never hated living in London,
I only hated living there with her.
A crevasse of hurt runs across her cheek,

but she puckers up, contents
herself by hurtling through
the locomotive's glass, "Let's
divorce." I toss my bags under the seat
as she yells, "Bastard," at me.

The train chugs slowly down
the tracks. Her bitter tongue does
not penetrate the window, merely
smudges it with spittle I can turn
away from. I can ignore.

In November 1961 Sylvia was awarded a Eugene Saxton Grant of $2,000 to write prose fiction to be delivered in four installments over the next year. She delivered to the Saxton Foundation what would be published as *The Bell Jar*. At the time she was awarded the Saxton, *The Bell Jar* was mostly written and had already been signed (on October 21, 1961) to be published in Britain by Heinemann under the pseudonym Victoria Lucas.

Mania

Aurelia Plath
October 1962

Sylvia's letters terrify
and so I telegram Winifred Davies,
her midwife, nurse, and friend.
I ask Winifred to find Sylvia good help,

a proper nanny for whom I will pay.
My Sivvy's back on that pendulum,
swings from her high genius
who composes brilliant poems

before Baby Nick's first morning cry
to her low immobile slug,
that cave of disgust and exhaustion.
I beg her to come home.

I want to stretch my arms across the ocean,
shelter my baby and my grandbabies.
But Sivvy's stubbornness
won't be undone. A vault of iron,

she can't be cracked.
She hurls her venom at me—
how dare I interfere, how dare I care.
I thought being a mother herself,

Sivvy would understand, but she
dives and flies so fast, so furious,
that she loses touch with herself
as mother and daughter,

becomes the writer, the great artist,
the loner. I bite my pen,
what should I do?
What can I do when I'm so far away?

Sylvia wrote her mother this alarming letter, dated October 16, 1962, which can be found in *Letters Home: Correspondence 1950–1963*:

"I need help very much now. Home is impossible. I can go nowhere with the children, and I am ill, and it would be psychologically the worst thing to see you now or to go home."

Part of Them

Susan O'Neill Roe, Sylvia's favorite nanny
October 1962

Sylvia treats me as a daughter
and a sister and a friend.

And I love Frieda and Nick
the first moment I hold them.

Sylvia is lovely, frail, wild, and brilliant.
I have never met a woman like her.

She doesn't hide emotions.
She pours it all onto the table

when the vase tumbles,
the mess and the flowers.

She needs me like a sick child,
like the nurse I am schooling to become.

I love her like my mother,
like my sister, like my friend,

like I am part of them.

Susan O'Neill Roe, a twenty-two-year-old found by Winifred Davies, started working for Sylvia on October 22, 1962. She was a mother's helper for Sylvia until mid-December, when Sylvia moved to London. Susan was studying to become a nurse.

Thirtieth Birthday

Imagining Sylvia Plath
*   In the style of "Ariel"*
*   October 27, 1962*

She writes
Into the cauldron of morning.
Eyes red, hands furious.

She does not blow out candles.
She lights them, grateful
For the mania of language,

For the fire-red poppies
Lifting their skirts.
They curtsy for her, bid her welcome

To a new decade.
There is no man in this house
Anymore. Only ladies and babies.

She can make a world of this.
He cannot. She can ride alone.
He cannot.

She rides her horse, Sam, ragged,
Clutches his mane.
When he bucks, she holds on,

Embeds her thighs
Into his back.
She is strong-legged.

She never knew she was this strong.
She blazes into sunrise.
She arrives, a woman of thirty.

Her mind unloads its words.
She must write it all down
Before the day unravels

Its fury and magic,
And she wakes, a sweet nymph,
A slave, a creature of air,

Fading quickly into ether.

"Ariel" demonstrates Sylvia's keen insight into her own art, reversing the prior death-in-birth obsession that had haunted her life. Out of those ashes, in the same early-morning hours that used to bring her such despair, Sylvia was now creating art, not suicide. Ariel was the name of the horse Sylvia rode in Croton, and the poem refers to the almost fatal ride Sylvia had on a horse named Sam when she was at Cambridge.

London at the End of October

A. Alvarez, poetry editor of the Observer
1962

We sip whiskey.
Sylvia squats beside the fire
as there is nowhere proper
to sit in my little studio flat.

She tells me that she
and Ted have separated.

I slug back a good portion
of whiskey, don't reveal
that Ted spends many nights
on my sofa.

Her eyes have closed.
She talks of writing her latest poems,

a woman possessed by demons
and angels, a muse to herself.
She produces a sheaf of poems
from her black shoulder bag,

says they must be read aloud.
I inch closer to her as she reads.

Her voice like the pied piper,
raw and wicked, draws me in.
I tell her she is writing strong
and new work—poems that amaze.

The poems Sylvia read to Alvarez were later published in *Ariel*, including "Berck-Plage," "The Moon and the Yew Tree," and "Elm."

Divorce

Suzette Macedo, a friend of both Assia's and Sylvia's
Late October 1962

Sylvia sobs in her sleep,
announces her intent to
divorce Ted as though

we are telephone
lines to his ear. I want to
cup her in my palm

like a baby bird.
She is that frantic, wild-winged,
with a fragile bald head

and a starving, gaping beak.
I restrain myself from phoning Assia,
from holding the mouthpiece

above Sylvia's loud tears
so Assia can hear
what unbearable sounds like.

Though English divorce rates generally climbed during the post-war years, divorce was not considered common in 1961. That year, there were 27,224 divorces in England.

Her Poetry

Peter Orr, interviewer of Sylvia and recorder of her poems
Late October 1962

Her voice older than her birth years,
controlled intonations—

she lets the punch of her words
catch one's attention. Her voice is merely

a shop window's dummy
displaying a dashing new frock of words.

She has been a professional
poet since she was eight,

admires the other confessionalists,
Lowell and Sexton, and challenges

always that her own work must transcend
the personal, be relevant,

not a shut box, not mirror-looking.
Her poetry is essential to her,

like bread or air. Nothing, she says,
is more fulfilling than writing a poem.

"Nothing?" I question her.
"Nothing," she affirms.

She does not speak of husbands
or children, thank God, only of verse.

Orr's interview, which included Sylvia's reading of her poems, was recorded for the British Council and the British Broadcasting Company's archives. Sylvia's reading of "Berck-Plage" was also recorded for a program called *The Weird Ones*, which aired on November 17, 1962.

Finally, a New Home

Susan O'Neill Roe, Frieda and Nick's nanny
November 1962

She hums over the collected poems
of William Butler Yeats, the green
bound volume in front of her
as she sits cross-legged before the fire.

I see how much she needs magic to happen,
desperate as a child wishing
St. Nick to bring her Christmas bicycle, Sylvia
pines for a sign that Yeats's old flat is meant for her.

She flips open the volume,
her finger catches on the page
containing *The Unicorn from the Stars*.
She lights up like a flare

suddenly flamed, streaking sparks.
Her forefinger quivers
and she reads me the line
sent to her by the master poet:

"Get the wine and food
to give you strength and courage
and I will get the house ready."
And there it is, the miracle she requires,

the London flat will be hers, it is destined,
tea-leaved, preordained by the stars.
I exhale, my departure now eased
because the city will care for her.

She will not be isolated
on acres of frost and silence.
I pick up her teacup, head upstairs
before Baby Nick begins my day.

There was a blue plaque to denote that the house at 23 Fitzroy Road was a historic London structure. It read, "William Butler Yeats 1865–1939 Irish Poet & Dramatist Lived Here," alongside the sign announcing, "Flat for Let." Sylvia had long admired Yeats's poetry. He was one of her favorites, and she felt that she was meant to live in his apartment. Sylvia also believed that she could communicate with Yeats's spirit.

November of Rejection and Rage

Imagining Sylvia Plath
In the style of "Winter Trees"
November 1962

Will these poems dissolve, blotted ink
On a journal page? She knows this work of *Ariel*
Exceeds her previous poems, published so readily,
But when huddled into a volume, received winter-cold.
Her *Colossus* fades under-read, buried on the library shelf
Beneath a blanket of snowy indifference.

The magazine editors brutalize her new poems.
Too extreme, bitchy language, personal squawks.
Her novel, *The Bell Jar,* rejected by American publishers,
Written under pseudonym, because her semi-
     autobiographical
"Potboiler" might scald her loved ones.
Every day the post delivers another "No," another ego
     blow.

November rages in her throat. She cannot hear
The name Ted without cracking and hissing
Like burning leaves. She chants ill will to the bastard,
To the deadbeat dad. She wonders how she failed at
     marriage,
Failed at bringing her poetry into the world.
Still she writes.

"Winter Trees" is part of the collection *Winter Trees* and is included in *The Collected Poems*. The poem examines the effortless way a tree seeds, even in winter, and contrasts it to the barren feelings Sylvia suffered at this time.

Moving

Susan O'Neill Roe, Sylvia's favorite nanny
December 10, 1962

The Morris loaded full as a stuffed bird,
we fight the December wind
all the way to London.
The children howl in the backseat.

No heat, no gas, no apartment keys.
No help from her downstairs neighbor,
the scruffy Mr. Trevor Thomas. This does not
bode well for Sylvia's promised city.

She wearies from slogging the kids
up two flights of stairs. Prams and nappies
and bottles—cold and flu running their noses
and temperatures. Sylvia may not be able to go this alone.

I fear for her, but then the gas boys show up,
jimmy open a window, and let her in.
Sylvia begins to settle, paints her furniture
white, nests into her home.

She tells me Ted often stops by.
Her voice on the phone tight as a fist
when she intones his name. She tells me
she is not alone. She has friends.

But I hear in her voice a hollow,
solitary note. A quiet cry for help
beyond what I'm able to provide.

Susan O'Neill Roe attended nursing school in January 1963 in London. Susan and her boyfriend, Corin Hughes-Stanton, treated Sylvia to the movies in mid-January.

At the Zoo

Ted Hughes
December 12, 1962

I pick Sylvia and Frieda and Nick
up from the Fitzroy Road flat,
steer Nicholas's pram
over to the London Zoo.

Frieda hunches over, scratches
her armpits in front of the ape house.
I storm her, the daddy gorilla,
hoot in front of the glass cage.

Sylvia's eyes burn crimson,
no tears, but she looks like she might cry.
We play family. Sylvia dances, then fumes.
One moment her hand on the pushchair

with mine, the next she jerks it away
and refuses to speak to me.
Mad as a feral cat caught in a trap,
she straightens Nick's stocking hat,

looks up at me. Frieda kicks, perched
on top of my shoulders. And then I see it,
desire floods Sylvia's cheeks.
Alvarez warned me about Sylvia's desperate

wish for reconciliation.
Like a burned-out bulb, she tries
but can't flash light. Her need flickers,
betrays her safety-pinned lips.

In part of her introduction to *Letters Home*, Aurelia offers that in letters and phone calls Sylvia conveyed to her that she was both furious with Ted and wanted a reconciliation. It is unclear what the actual legal status of her marriage/separation/divorce with Ted was at this time and up until Sylvia's death. In a letter to her mother dated October 12, 1962, Sylvia writes, ". . . Ted does want the divorce, thank goodness, so it shouldn't be difficult." And according to Clement Moore (Warren's friend and old roommate at Exeter), in Butscher's *Sylvia Plath: Method and Madness*, Moore's stepfather called Sylvia in late October to make sure that Sylvia had legal advice, and at that time a formal divorce was presumably planned. No paperwork has surfaced pertaining to the divorce.

Ted was with Assia in December 1962 but was also dating a few models. By most accounts both Ted and Sylvia considered themselves legally separated.

Temptation

A. Alvarez, poetry editor of the Observer
December 1962

She visits my studio Thursday afternoons
the last couple months. She fills her
cocktail glass a few too many times,
crouches on the red carpet,

smokes her cigarettes
without inhaling, a neophyte
to the art. Eventually, she opens
her black portfolio and reads her work.

Languorous, deliberate, her words
ax and burn. They sound
smooth and pointed, icicles
on the roof's ledge.

Sylvia drops tears from the edge,
I am mesmerized by her.
But she mistakes admiration
for something more,

places her hand on my inner thigh,
tests how warm my water runs.
I don't tell her that I'm loyal
to friends, or that I have met

a new woman who stops my pulse.
I just ignore Sylvia's unspoken proposal,
play ignorant. I long,
like a moth, to fly

from Sylvia's space,
out the glass window. But I hit
the pane, bounce back into the room,
summoned by the light of her poetry.

I circle her beacon voice.
I can't help myself. She is that
raw, that good—her bold bee
series dazzles.

The poem she reads today,
"Daddy," breaks me apart
like eggshell. It's obvious
that Ted shattered Sylvia,

that she'll never be whole again,
that he played her daddy, let her down
hard as stone. I refuse to involve myself
in the muck of their affair.

I sip my bourbon, keep my hands
folded over my lap,
and try not to look at her
full red lips.

Sylvia probably considered the "Bee" poems her best work, placing them near the end of *Ariel*. If the importance of the "Bee" sequence was once overlooked, it may be partly because Hughes moved the poems to the middle of *Ariel* when he put together his version for the book's initial publication. Sylvia wrote the five "Bee" poems between October 3 and October 9, 1963, during the breakup of her marriage.

The "Bee" poems are connected not only by their subject matter, but also by their five-line stanza pattern. They deal with Sylvia's father and Sylvia's ascendance as her family's queen bee, but also with the relationship between the poems' narrator and her world.

Professor Karen Ford of the University of Oregon explains: "The sequence moves from community, in 'The Bee Meeting,' to solitude, in 'Wintering,' as the speaker settles her relations with others and with her own former selves."

Inconsiderate

Trevor Thomas, Sylvia's downstairs neighbor at Fitzroy Road
December 1962

Ill and ill-mannered,
she stole the second-floor flat
from me and my sons
with her green American dollars.

I implore her thrice to keep
the entranceway clean, not clogged
with baby toys and debris.
I know she stuffs my bin with her rubbish.

Under her breath she calls *me* ill-tempered.
The hall is not a garage, I say to her.
If she finds me unkind for pointing this out,
then her manners need mending.

What kind of mother taught her
to abuse her neighbors like this—taught her
to be a rude American, thinking a smile
and a plea will get her out of anything.

Trevor Thomas was an artist who worked as a fine arts editor at the Gordon Fraser Gallery. Trevor was divorced and the father of two sons. He had wanted to move into the upper flat, but Sylvia offered more money and beat him out. Relations between Trevor Thomas and Sylvia improved somewhat when he discovered that she was Sylvia Plath, the poet. Also, as Sylvia slipped further into depression and despair, Trevor softened and took pity on her.

Victoria Lucas

Trevor Thomas, Sylvia's downstairs neighbor at Fitzroy Road
January 1963

A strange bird, a regular
toucan. When she refuses
to answer the front bell,
I howl wind and wolf up the stairs.
She flies open the door,
yells louder than any polite woman,
"Can't you see I'm ill? I want to see
no one. I have so much to do."

A few days later, Sylvia pounds
on my door. I see her through
the peephole and almost pretend
to be away, but she's crying.
My heart's no boulder, so I unlatch
the door. She melts onto the sofa.
She says she's going to die,
and who will mind the children?

She blubbers and fumes, gives me
a blushworthy account
of her marriage's dissolve.
Her anger smokes the parlor,
"That awful woman, that Jezebel."
Sylvia steams, blames them both.
I stare at the grandfather clock
behind her head, wonder how

many minutes more this will last,
what excuse I might proffer
to escape? Sylvia flips open
the *Observer*, points to a poem
her husband wrote, then to a review
of a new book, *The Bell Jar*.
Mrs. Hughes claims she wrote it
under the pseudonym Victoria Lucas.

The name was all Ted. Victoria for Ted's
favorite cousin, Vicky Farrar, and Lucas
for that bastard friend of Ted's, Lucas Myers.
Lucas never did like her, never gave her
a chance. She rocks on the davenport,
whispers that her name
is Sylvia Plath. I choke on my tea—
I recognize that byline—

who knew that Mrs. Hughes was Miss Plath?
I digest this as she bursts tear balloons,
shivers and quakes on my sofa.
She is a curious bird indeed—
a cuckoo, a dodo, a peacock
just now fanning open her feathers.
She looks entirely different to me
now. I reach out and touch her hand.

This incident is recorded in the unpublished memoirs of Trevor Thomas and in
Paul Alexander's *Rough Magic*.

Apparition at Window

Valerie St. Johnson, across-the-street neighbor,
her son plays with Frieda and Nick
January 1963

She stands, no motion
in her limbs, looking for him.
Hours before he comes,

hours after he leaves.
He haunts her. His dark figure
turns the corner of her

mind black and blank. He
freezes her feet to the floor.
He disappears. Her

husband, black-scarved. She
starves for him. Perhaps I should
say something to her, but

what? Ask her to step
away from the window, stop
longing for a ghost?

Valerie St. Johnson's account can be found in Paul Alexander's *Rough Magic* and is based on his interview with the St. Johnsons.

Friends who were close to both Ted and Sylvia generally tried to not actively take sides during the separation. But from most accounts, those who came in contact with Sylvia during this time felt sympathy for her and her predicament.

Letter for the Future

Aurelia Plath
      February 4, 1963

Sivvy catalogs
her future, writes that friends will
visit, and she has

summer travel plans,
work on the BBC. She
admits she's grim as

London rain. That her
marriage is dead as winter trees.
But I dare not fret,

Dr. Horder found
her a therapist, prescribed
her new pills. Things will

improve. By spring we'll
giggle over this winter's
cold. Things will be fine.

I balance myself, one
hand on the frosty windowpane.
Something in Sivvy's letter

knocks out my breath.
My lungs can't hold air, my exhales
don't register on the window's glass.

The letter dated February 4, 1963, is the last included in *Letters Home*. While not exactly chipper, the letter does discuss Sylvia's plans for the next several months as though things were improving for her. The letter ends: "I am going to start seeing a woman doctor, which should help me weather this difficult time. Give my love to all. Sivvy."

Breaking Point

Sylvia's London au pair
February 1963

Crazy, that's what she is,
knocks me down
with the back of her hand,
demands I leave
without goodbye to the little ones,
without my pay.

Oh, she'll regret it,
that Mrs. Hughes. She thinks
I do nothing.

She'll see
when her hands are deep
in nappies,
her fingers frozen by
the faucet's cold drip.
She'll see all I do for her.

She rings me,
begs me to return.
Please, she needs help.

True as night
she needs help,
but she'll not get it from me,
she can drive herself
straight to hell
as far as I'm concerned.

Sylvia told two separate stories about this incident with the au pair; one was that
the au pair quit for no reason, and the second was that Sylvia fired the au pair because she had left the children alone. Sylvia related the incident in which she refused to pay the au pair and assaulted her to her friend Jillian Becker.

Dysfunction

Jillian Becker, a writer and friend of Sylvia's
February 8, 1963

Hysterical at
my doorstep, no coats on the
children. No clothes, no

bottles. She melts, hands
me little Nick, will I help
her, watch them, she's sick,

she can't eat or sleep.
The children will die. Please help,
please let her lie down.

I tuck her in like
a child, wait until the
pills carry her off

to sleep, to Lethe, past
the kill hours, the clock just
before dawn. Sleep saves

her, she gorges my
toast and eggs. Frieda tugs at
her sleeve. But Syl can't

see her. I phone Syl's
doctor, what should I do? He
says there are no beds

in the hospital—
that she is wait-listed, that
I should force her to

care for her children,
that her love for them will save
Sylvia. But when

I hand her Nick, the
nipple in his mouth, Syl drops
the bottle, glass shards

the tile. Nick in tears.
Frieda bites her thumb. My kids
retreat, silenced. They

puzzle over this
woman of cardboard, too weak
to feed her baby.

Now I need help, my
husband at work, my floor drenched
with spilled milk. My hands

shake. I don't know how
to help her. She asks me to
fetch her party dress.

She has a date that
night, don't wait up for her. She
takes the keys. She's gone!

Jillian Becker wrote a book about Sylvia's final few days called *Giving Up: The Last Days of Sylvia Plath.*

Saturday Night

Ted Hughes
February 9, 1963

Was I dreaming, did
Sylvia meet me dressed
in her silver skirt, curled
hair, lips righteous red
with the stain of her blood?

Did she bite my neck,
ask to start over
like that day she first
drew my blood?
Did I tell her
that Assia is pregnant?
Did I tell Sylvia
that I no longer loved her,
that she'd best move on?

Or did I enter her flat,
remove my soaked scarf,
and ask about Frieda and Nick?
Did Syl say she
had an engagement
and had to depart
as she examined my face
and her hand hovered
above my thigh?

Why did we meet? What did I
say? Where was the woman
I once called wife?
Did I whisper to a ghost?
Did I even see Sylvia at all?

Purportedly, Assia miscarried the child she was carrying at this time. Other accounts claim that she had an abortion shortly after Sylvia's death. This night was
the last time Ted saw Sylvia alive.

Taxi Driver

Gerry Becker, friend of Sylvia's, Jillian's husband
February 10, 1963

I slide into my donkey jacket,
adjust my fur hat, tie a butcher's
apron round my waist to protect
my clothes from the unwanted grease
of the steering wheel. I tuck
Sylvia, Frieda, and Nick into the backseat,
plant their meager bags at their feet.

This is what I do,
shuttle people place to place,
amuse them with friendly talk,
point out local sites of interest.
The glass between front and backseat
is thick, but cracked today,
so the kids feel more heat.

The twenty-mile drive is silent
as snow. But when I pause
at a red light, muffled over
the rough engine rumble I hear her,
weep and weep and weep.
I tell myself I am not a zookeeper,
no tamer of wild things.

Drivers don't ask why, you know,
we just take you where you want to go.
But Sylvia is my friend,
not a fare.
I pull the black cab over,
open the passenger door. The bitter wind
is a knife, but Sylvia doesn't flinch.

Her hands barely keep her head
from falling through the floorboards.
The little ones erupt into crying,
tears hard as diamonds.
I hold them on my knees,
plead with Sylvia, "Let me
take you back home with me."

She snaps out of her trance,
out of her teary-eyed jag.
She is resolved to return home,
says Jillian, and I have been more
than gracious. Our Irish nurse, Phyllis,
has tended Frieda and Nicholas long enough,
tonight they need their own beds.

I return to my position
as chauffeur. When we arrive
at the Fitzroy Road flat,
Nick snores soundly. Frieda and Sylvia
sit on top of each other
like a Madonna and Child marble frieze,
red-eyed, tearstained, stone tangled with stone.

I do not want to leave them,
I invite myself in for tea.
I seem to cheer her. She talks about the future
as though it were a bright, clear day.
I grow tired, promise to drop in tomorrow.
When I climb into my cab it smells different,
stale, sour, and it's cold as a ghost.

Besides Sylvia's children and her downstairs neighbor, Trevor Thomas, Gerry Becker was the last person, and certainly the last friend, to see Sylvia alive and to witness her state of mind. Gerry's account is well documented by his wife, Jillian, in her book *Giving Up*.

Sunday Night, Monday Morning

Trevor Thomas, Sylvia's downstairs neighbor at Fitzroy Road
February 10–11, 1963

Eleven-forty-five p.m.
and rat-a-tat-tat
on my door,
Sylvia wonders
if I have airmail stamps
she can buy.

I tell her calmly
that the post
won't be picked up
until tomorrow,
when she can buy
her own stamps.

"But no," she slurs,
"I want to put the letters
in the box tonight."
Sylvia staggers,
medication
on her breath.

No point in arguing,
I hand her my stamps,
refuse her payment.
She stomps her foot,
sighs, "No.
I must pay you

or I won't be right
with my conscience
before God, will I?"
Well, hell's bells,
if I didn't find her
a strange bird before.

Whatever that Dr. Horder prescribes
makes her hatter mad tonight.
Sylvia asks what time
I leave for work.
I scratch my elbow, tell her
half past eight.

We lock gazes
and I almost invite
her in for a drink
to calm her down,
but the hour's late
and I'm a working man.

I bid her well,
bolt the door.
Ten minutes pass
and Sylvia stands
in the same place,
stamps in hand.

She peers up
at the lightbulb
like it is the Star
of Bethlehem.
I'm in my stockings,
but I open the door.

I inform her
that I'm phoning
Dr. Horder. She smiles
like a babe, radiant,
pleads, "Oh no,
I'm just having

a marvelous dream,
a most wonderful
vision." Befuddled
and cold in the hallway,
I blow on my hands
and close the door.

I convince myself
that she seems happy
and shuffle into bed.
But I can't rightly sleep.
Sylvia bangs about
upstairs, her feet run

like mice in the walls,
no, more like elephants
on stampede. Clump-
clump-bang. Were
it not below freezing
I'd ring her bell

and tell her the racket
must cease. God sakes,
it's half past midnight.
But thankfully
her feet or something
rhythms me to sleep.

This account of Trevor Thomas's interaction with Sylvia right before her death
comes from interviews the biographer Paul Alexander conducted with Thomas
and is recorded in Alexander's *Rough Magic*.

Winter's End

Imagining Sylvia Plath
  In the style of "Edge"
  February 11, 1963

She is determined, ready as a knife,
Her letters sealed.

The hall light smiles, a halo calling her
To flame. She wings into the kitchen,

Spreads mustard on their crustless bread,
Pours two pure white glasses of milk.

She kisses the children's foreheads,
Folds over their sheets.

The streetlamp clicks off.
She opens the window to dawn,

Wedges a towel under the children's door.
Righteous, happy as a rose,

She knows her place in the garden.
Her black petals curl underground.

She tidies her desk, leaves her manuscript,
Ariel and Other Poems, to the moon,

To the world of bone. The sun breaks
Like yolk. It is time.

She unlatches the oven door. The gas
Fills her nostrils, sweet as blood, pungent as a sword.

"Edge" is the final poem in *Ariel* as the collection was first arranged by Ted and
initially published. (Sylvia intended *Ariel* to end with the poem "Wintering.")
"Edge" focuses on the image of a dead mother and her two dead children. Written
on February 5, 1963, it is a chilling, exquisitely crafted work and perhaps the last
poem Sylvia wrote.

Monday Morning

Myra Norris, nurse hired to care for Frieda and Nick
February 11, 1963

Nine sharp and I ring all the bells,
can't read the patient's name
on any box, covered as they are in frost.

Not a soul answers my buzzing.
It's as if the whole building sleeps,
spellbound like Sleeping Beauty's kingdom.

I phone my agency. They confirm
that I've the right address,
23 Fitzroy Road.

I circle the building, hear a small
cry like a hungry baby bird,
whimpering from the second-floor window.

As I round the corner, the cry
turns to a roar loud as a midnight
wolf. It's the children screaming.

I dash to find help, anyone big
who can break down doors. A builder,
a Mr. Langridge, wrenches off the front-door lock.

We smell it right away, gas,
cover our mouths with kerchiefs,
leap the stairs two at a time.

Inside the flat, we rush to turn off the gas,
Mrs. Hughes's head inside the oven
like another awful fairy tale, the one

where the witch dies inside the stove.
We pull her into the front room
and I push on her heart, blow

all my breath into her mouth,
but she's stiff-limbed, pale purple,
without pulse, without air.

Mr. Langridge rescues the children
from their frozen beds, swaddles them
in blankets, and carries them from the flat.

One match and the whole building
could have gone up
like a mushroom cloud.

Sylvia's body was discovered sometime after nine a.m. Dr. Horder identified her body for the coroner, and Ted claimed it on February 15, 1963. He took it to Yorkshire to be buried in his family's cemetery in Heptonstall.

The Hughes children were freezing that morning but did not suffer from exposure to the gas. Trevor Thomas, however, almost died of carbon monoxide poisoning, as the gas had seeped down into his room and knocked him out as he slept. He did not wake until the afternoon and was then taken to the hospital.

Failure

Dr. Horder, Sylvia's London doctor, and Dr. Beuscher,
Sylvia's American therapist
February 1963

1. Him

February, the most terrible month,
a cold so complete I have nothing

good to wake for. The phone
that morning pierces me like a bullet.

Stunned, I toss on my shoes,
grab my doctor's bag,

and open the door to death,
to man's professional failure.

Sylvia was a hospital bed away from help.
I should have tucked her under my own covers,

but I am a limited man. A doctor,
I suppose, is saddled with limits.

I can't cry over her death, but the rage
inside knifes at my heart.

2. Her

When you act against your heart
and mind, only dumb luck

can save you. My luck dries up.
I have given up sleep

like it is a present I don't deserve.
Sylvia haunts me when I close my eyes,

she says, "Don't worry, Dr. Ruth.
I will be fine. I am fine."

After Sylvia's death, Ruth was deeply sad and plagued by guilt. When she sought professional counsel, a senior therapist told Ruth that Sylvia's death was not her fault, that in fact Ruth had likely kept her alive five or six extra years. When Ruth divorced her second husband, she burned a lot of things, including Sylvia's letters, which she later regretted. Ruth devoted much of her life to maintaining an accurate portrait of Sylvia as she saw her. Ruth died in 1999, poor, depressed, and before she could go on her much-anticipated Alaskan cruise, a cruise she sold her signed first edition of *The Colossus* to take.

What She Left Behind

Ted Hughes
February 1963

The carbon she left
on her desk of *Ariel*
will leave a fossil record.

She read me only
a few of these poems.
I hold the papers, astonished.

She did not tell me
what she wanted to do
with these last words,
publish them, perish with them,
or both.

Her poetry cuts me to the spine,
beautiful and brutal.
Her words startle my eyes.
She has etched down parts of me,
of us, of her.

Her voice records its final,
triumphant symphony.
And I know, slumped
over her desk, my head
so heavy in my hands

I can barely read her lines,
that it was either her or me,
one of us had to go.

Ariel was published in 1965 at Ted's behest, first in Britain by Faber and Faber and then in 1966 in America by Harper & Row. Ted did not use Sylvia's previous publishers because he secured a better deal with his own British publisher, Faber and Faber, and negotiated a more profitable contract with Harper & Row as well. Ted removed some poems and rearranged the order of the poems included in the first editions of *Ariel*, but subsequent printings of the collection are truer in their arrangement to Sylvia's intentions.

Ted and Assia remained together for nearly seven years. On March 25, 1969, Assia killed herself and the daughter, Shura, whom she had with Ted. After taking sleeping pills and dissolving some in water for Shura, she gassed herself and the child in their kitchen. Assia was forty-one and Shura was four at the time of their deaths. Ted and Assia never married, and by some accounts he was planning at this time to marry Carol Orchard, who became his second wife and stepmother to Nick and Frieda.

Funeral

Margaret Plath, Sylvia's sister-in-law, Warren's wife
February 16, 1963

Ted arrives in the same black car
as her coffin,
snow remnants glimmer off the tires.

Ted chose this burial place,
Heptonstall, beside the moors,
where his family rots underground.

So few people in attendance:
the Beckers, Ted's parents,
a local churchgoer named Joan,
Ted, Warren, and me.

You'd think Sylvia was a social
recluse, all those guests she welcomed
to her home, all those men
who published her work
missing like pages torn from a journal.

Ted's sister is down with the flu,
Frieda and Nicholas are too young
for this horror, and Aurelia
hasn't the strength to fly.

The rector's spectacles glare.
No friend to Sylvia or Ted,
he reads scripture about lilies
and valleys. I clutch Warren's arm.

I did not get to know Sylvia,
though I wanted to. I wish now
that Warren had sailed me
across the Atlantic a few months ago
when Sylvia SOS'ed for my help.

I would have picked up her babies
when her arms grew weak,
held her hand when her words
failed her.

In the cemetery
the snow hides most of the markers
of death. A brown, moist hole
in the ground where Sylvia
will be laid.
It is so silent
the wind stops its whirl.

Warren's eyes
hold a pain I have never
before seen,
a vacancy beyond torture,
with no hope for release.
I purse my lips in silence,
there is nothing I can say.

After the burial Ted tells us
that Sylvia's gravestone will read
"Sylvia Plath Hughes 1932–1963,"
with the inscription:
"Even amidst fierce flames
the golden lotus can be planted."

Warren and I nod,
there is nothing we can say.

The epitaph on Sylvia's headstone comes from the book *Monkey*, written by Wu Ch'Eng-En in the sixteenth century. Spoken by a patriarch who is teaching Monkey the best way to live a long life, the full quotation is: "To spare and tend the vital powers, this and nothing else is sum and total of all magic, secret and profane. All is comprised in these three, Spirit, Breath and Soul; guard them closely, screen them well; let there be no leak. Store them within the frame; that is all that can be learnt, and all that can be taught. I would have you mark the tortoise and snake, locked in tight embrace. Locked in tight embrace, the vital powers are strong; even in the midst of fierce flames the Golden Lotus may be planted, the Five Elements compounded and transposed, and put to new use. When that is done, be which you please, Buddha or Immortal."

Silent as the Snow

Warren Plath
February 16, 1963

Strangers in a half crescent
around the hole that will
hold my sister's body.

They look at me like
I should pull words
of comfort from my jacket pocket
for them.

But my mourning is private,
a vault I seal here
at her grave.

Warren Plath became an executive in the research division of IBM. After Sylvia's death, he never communicated his experiences with or feelings about her publicly.

Posthumous

Aurelia Plath
February 1963

Grief, my dears,
is a necklace choked
around my neck.

They say there's nothing
worse than the loss of a child
and I concur.

I buried a husband
too soon. And now I remain
an ocean away as they lower Sivvy

under foreign earth. My heart
rains enough tears
to flood the Atlantic.

I can still feel Sylvia's first kick
in my gut. I will never
lose the feeling.

I clutch the letters, bundled
in ribbon and string, that I have
stowed away all these years.

I straighten her books on my shelf,
stare at that last photograph snapped
of Sylvia, Frieda, and Nick.

Oh, the masterworks she birthed.

Letters from friends and admirers torrent in.
I expect the postman will never stop
delivering them until I, too, lie underground.

Oh, my darling, my dearest,
my child, I failed to help you
in life. I pray for the strength

to do right for you in death—
to remember your smiles,
your curls—to love you daily

through your boy and your girl,
to bring your words into the world
so they might do some good,

might save someone
lost, keep her breathing,
keep her head above the tide.

Aurelia was forbidden to publish Sylvia's letters until 1975, lest she risk never seeing her grandchildren. Ted briefly considered letting Aurelia raise Frieda and Nick, but he opted instead to move back to Court Green and have Olwyn, his sister, "mother" them.

Olwyn not only mothered the children, but also managed Sylvia's literary estate. Few biographies existed about Sylvia until the last twenty years, because Olwyn and/or Ted often demanded the ability to edit the biography (as Olwyn did with Anne Stevenson's *Bitter Fame*) or else they denied biographers' requests to see Sylvia's work and journals or have permission to reprint her fiction and poetry. Ted Hughes remained silent on the subject of Sylvia, never granting interviews, until 1998 when he published *Birthday Letters*.

Ted destroyed the last journal Sylvia kept during the final months of her life, partly because he thought it would hurt their children. Dr. Beuscher burned the letters Sylvia wrote her. So several pieces of Sylvia's life remain unknown. The largest collections of Sylvia's writing are housed at Smith College and at Indiana University.

Your Own, Sylvia

Imagining Sylvia Plath
In the style of "Child"

She could not help burning herself
From the inside out,
Consuming herself

Like the sun.
But the memory of her light blazes
Our dark ceiling.

She could not know how long
Her luminary would map the sky,
Or where her dying would lead the lost.

But for those who gaze heavenly
Or into the reflected pool of night,
She is fuel. She is dust. She is a guiding star.

Written on January 28, 1963, "Child" is about motherhood. Composed for her children, the poem catalogs what Sylvia wished to bestow upon them and what she hoped to shield them from. "Child" can be found in both *Winter Trees* and *The Collected Poems*. Sylvia Plath is an influential presence not only in the bookstore, library, and classroom, but also in the vast realms of cyberspace. There are blogs, teen discussion sites, and Web sites devoted entirely to her life and work. One of the best is www.sylviaplathforum.com.

Dear Reader,

It's hard to explain exactly why I love Sylvia Plath. I know that I felt sparks, almost like a jolt of static electricity, when my best friend first read me Sylvia's poem "Edge." At fifteen I had this dark, fierce place inside me that no one quite understood and that I myself couldn't articulate. I found my way to *Ariel*, and in those pages it seemed as if Sylvia read my mind, wrote from the black cavern of my heart. Her words were more than real. They were fearless. A revelation.

As I researched Sylvia's work for this book, not only did I gain further admiration for her gifts of language and rhythm, her unique blend of autobiography and fiction, but also I found that again I related to her in an almost eerie way. Both of us were writers, both of us struggled with how to balance our art with our lives.

Another thing I came to understand was just how deep and widespread the kinship with Sylvia's life and writing has become. There is something about her raw honesty that makes you feel like you know her, understand her, are understood by her. Her words laser through boundaries of culture, age, and gender, to speak to our universal psyche. This unique bonding between Sylvia and her readers is one of the reasons why *Your Own, Sylvia* was chosen as the book's title.

My method for developing the book was to begin each day by taking a line from a Plath poem and journaling in poetry—writing out my thoughts and feelings starting with one of her images or ideas. I also sent my mother daily letters, as Sylvia often did. I wrote about my writing and my life. I tried to channel Sylvia, as well as the younger me reacting to Plath for the first time. Re-experiencing the tragedies and triumphs of her life and her art, I fell in love all over again. And then I began writing the poems for this novel.

This book, although based on real events and real people, is first and foremost a work of fiction. I have taken liberties imagining conversations and descriptions and interpreting the feelings of the real people speaking in these poems. My intention is to illuminate Sylvia Plath's life and work and to introduce newcomers to this astonishing poet and woman. I tried to do this with as much authenticity as possible and hope the results reflect this intention.

As to purpose, Sylvia questions it herself in her poem "The Night Dances." She wonders why she has been given:

> These lamps, these planets
> Falling like blessings, like flakes

For me the answer is clear: Sylvia was given the night sky's brilliance so her writing can be a light for all of us. Please go find her. Her writing is a gift—*The Bell Jar, Ariel, The Colossus, The Collected Poems,* her letters and journals. On these amazing pages you just might discover yourself.

Sincerely,

Stephanie Hemphill

Source Notes and Bibliography

Piecing together the life of Sylvia Plath was a daunting task. Sylvia is an artist I hold in high esteem and with whom I feel an affinity. Her life and work have fascinated many writers before me, and several conflicting accounts of her life exist. We know too that a portion of her work and some of the information about her life has been suppressed or destroyed, or, due to legal restrictions, may not be available for another decade or more. For these reasons it seemed best to convey my interpretation of Sylvia's story through the voices of the people who knew and experienced her and through the words and literature she left behind.

To acquire information for these perspectives, my research for this book was two-pronged. I read all of Sylvia's poetry and fiction, and as many of her journals and letters as I was able to get my hands on. I then relied on biographers and their interviews with the people who knew Sylvia to fill in the details of her life. The different voices of this book come primarily from three biographies: Edward Butscher's *Sylvia Plath: Method and Madness,* Anne Stevenson's *Bitter Fame,* and most significantly, Paul Alexander's *Rough Magic.*

The sociopolitical stance of the author or scholar at the time different biographies or articles were written on Plath often dictated the hue of the presentation of Sylvia's life. Sylvia has been taken up by feminists and formalists, by psychologists and journalists. She has been called a victim, a lunatic, a genius—in various combinations. I read biographies and articles on Plath written in different decades by scholars, friends, family members, and colleagues in order to have a more complete picture of Sylvia's importance and influence, and how she has been characterized and remembered, in the forty-plus years since her death.

When Sylvia died, her estate, including all of her fiction, articles, and journals, became the property of Ted Hughes. Ted assigned Olwyn, his sister, to be the executor of the Plath collections. Because the Hugheses refused interviews, denied would-be biographers access to essential documents, and turned down requests to quote Sylvia's work, it was nearly impossible to publish well-informed biographies on Plath.

I found it essential to read Edward Butscher's biography, *Sylvia Plath: Method and Madness* (1976), the first biography to be published about Plath. It takes a psychoanalytic look at Sylvia's life and work. When Edward Butscher published *Method and Madness,* neither Plath's letters nor her journals had been published, nor had any of her fiction except for *The Bell Jar.* The Hugheses did not endorse this book and opposed its publication. I used several voices and anecdotes from interviews Butscher conducted for my poems in *Your Own, Sylvia.*

Designed in many ways to counterbalance what, by 1989, the Plath Estate saw as Plath's mistaken posthumous reputation as a feminist martyr, Anne Stevenson's *Bitter Fame* presents a unique view of Sylvia. Anne Stevenson began her research in 1985, after *The Collected Poems* and an abridged version of Sylvia's journals were made available. Anne Stevenson actually worked in conjunction with, and with the approval of, Olwyn and Ted. Because of this, *Bitter Fame* is well documented and offers many details about Sylvia's life. It provided texture and context for *Your Own, Sylvia,* but I did not use it as my primary source.

Paul Alexander's *Rough Magic* guided the structure of *Your Own, Sylvia* by most often helping me to select which voice seemed most apt to tell Sylvia's story at different moments in her life. Written in 1991, this biography is not the most recent book on Plath, but it remains one of the most respected and comprehensive. Alexander interviewed everyone he could who knew Plath, some of whom are no longer with us. For me the Alexander biography, although clearly sympathetic to Sylvia, seems less biased than *Method and Madness* and *Bitter Fame.* Also, at the time it was written, Alexander had more uncensored information available to him than did Stevenson or Butscher.

Taken altogether, those three biographies provided me with a base of understanding of the emotional inner workings of Sylvia and the people who knew her. The other sources I have cataloged offered further and often more specific details about Sylvia's life. For instance,

Elaine Feinstein's *Ted Hughes: The Life of a Poet* explores Sylvia's relationship with Ted from a different perspective, as does Ted's own *Birthday Letters*. "Sylvia and Ruth," a Salon.com article by Karen Maroda, illuminates components of Sylvia's relationship with Dr. Ruth Barnhouse, her therapist. Jillian Becker's *Giving Up* provides a uniquely personal description of the last few days Sylvia was alive.

If biographies provided the skeleton voices for the verse portrait of Plath, this book's "Imagining Sylvia" poems were written under the guidance of Sylvia's own poetry. These poems correspond to poems Sylvia wrote, so the date indicated on each of my new poems corresponds very nearly, if not exactly, to the date when the original Plath poem was written (with a few exceptions). I adopted the style of the original Plath poem, maintained the topic of the original, and incorporated Sylvia's imagery into the new poems wherever possible.

Along with her poetry and prose, Sylvia's journals and letters allowed me to access her thoughts and feelings. Many biographers do not have autobiographical records of their subjects, and I am so grateful to have these passages from inside Sylvia's amazing, prolific mind. I owe anything that is good about the "Imagining Sylvia" poems directly to Sylvia herself.

This verse portrait is intended to be a stepping stone to encourage everyone to read or reread Sylvia Plath's work. The best way to understand this mysterious, captivating artist and woman is to read what she left behind. I hope this book leads you there.

More detailed source notes and a bibliography for further reading follow.

Source Notes

"Dearest, Darling, First Born"—Information about Aurelia is from Paul Alexander's *Rough Magic*.

"Bee-Keeper, Penny-Pincher, Professor, Master of the House"— The analysis of the relationship between Sylvia and her father is Butscher's. Sylvia writes about visiting her father's grave in her journal dated Monday, March 9, 1959.

"The Day She Learned to Swim" and "Hurricane"—Details about Sylvia's childhood and Marian Freeman's recollections of Sylvia are from *Rough Magic*.

"Point Shirley"—Butscher and Alexander detail the Schober's house at Point Shirley.

"Losing a Limb"—Description and medical records of Otto's illness can be found in *Rough Magic* and Anne Stevenson's *Bitter Fame*.

"Mother's Strength"—The exact time of Otto's death is from *Sylvia Plath: Method and Madness*. Aurelia's background comes from *Bitter Fame*.

"First Publication"—"Poem" and information about it can be found in *Sylvia Plath: Method and Madness*.

"Maître d'Hotel"—Stevenson and Butscher provide background details about Frank Schober.

"Outpatient"—Alexander provides details about Aurelia's illness. In the introduction to *Letters Home,* Aurelia Plath describes the ways in which she kept her daughter's correspondence.

"Selfish"—The relationship between Sylvia and Warren is described by Aurelia in the introduction to *Letters Home.*

"Best Friend"—Sylvia's childhood with Betsy Powley at Annie F. Warren Grammar School is chronicled in *Bitter Fame* and in the introduction to *Letters Home.*

"Boy Crazy"—Ruth Freeman was interviewed by Paul Alexander, and Sylvia's feelings of awkwardness during adolescence are recounted by Aurelia in the introduction to *Letters Home.*

"Crocketteer"—Paul Alexander provides a lot of details about Wilbury Crockett and Sylvia's high school experience.

"Demolition"—Sylvia writes about her struggles with boys and sexuality in *The Journals of Sylvia Plath*. Bruce Elwell's experience of Sylvia comes from *Rough Magic*.

"A Room of Her Own"—Aurelia details the relationship between Warren and Sylvia in her introduction to *Letters Home*.

"Heartbreaker" and "Valedictorian"—Accounts of Sylvia's high school experience come from Paul Alexander's book.

"Lookout Farm" and "Paper Doll"—Sylvia writes about her experience at Lookout Farm and her relationship with Eddie Cohen in *The Journals of Sylvia Plath*.

"Dropout"—Ann Davidow's account comes from Anne Stevenson, and Sylvia writes about Ann in her journals.

"Patriarchy," "Tuberculosis," "Ski Trip," and "Stalemate"— Descriptions of Sylvia's dating life and relationship with Dick Norton come from Paul Alexander and her journals.

"Patient"—Anne Stevenson tracks Sylvia's lifelong struggle with sinusitis.

"Summer Job 1952"—Mr. Driscoll's memories of Sylvia come from *Rough Magic*.

"Job Number Two"—Sylvia recounts her experience with the Cantors in her journals, and Paul Alexander adds to the description of this experience in his biography.

"Proud" and "Aid"—*Rough Magic* and *The Journals of Sylvia Plath* paint portraits of Sylvia's lifelong benefactor Olive Higgins Prouty.

"The Caliber of Her Dating Pool," "Pretty, Tall, Crippled," "Golden Girl," "Marriage," "Darling, Darling," and "Farewell Boys"— Alexander tracks Sylvia's dating life at Smith.

"Pleasure," "Excellence," and "Stigmata"—Sylvia describes her experience at *Mademoiselle* in her journals and letters. Paul Alexander fills in the details of this experience through his interviews. Butscher paints a picture of Cyrilly Abels.

"Home Bitter Home"—Sylvia's journals describe her return home after her guest editorship.

"Shock Treatment," "Doctor-Patient Relations: Trial and Error," "Doctor's Notes," and "Debate"—Sylvia's treatment before and after her 1953 suicide attempt and Aurelia's reaction to it come from Paul Alexander.

"Suicide Watch"—The newspaper accounts of what happened to Sylvia come from *Bitter Fame* and *Sylvia Plath: Method and Madness.*

"Iconic," "Recommendation," "Bragging Rights," and "Put Your Studies to Good Use"—Butscher and Alexander detail Sylvia's Smith years.

"Abecedarian," "Debate," and "Madness"—Wilbury Crockett's aid to Sylvia is described in *Sylvia Plath: Method and Madness,* as well as some of the treatments employed during her stay at McLean.

"Blond Ambition" and "Twins"—Nancy Hunter's impressions about Sylvia derive from Paul Alexander's *Rough Magic* and Ronald Hayman's *The Death and Life of Sylvia Plath.*

In large part, Paul Alexander provides the context for Sylvia's Cambridge years and the people she knew while she studied there.

Butscher, Stevenson, and Alexander provided details about Sylvia and Ted's relationship, as well as most of the sources suggested for further reading.

"Complaints" and "Their Flat Creaks and Cries, 'Money, Money' "— These accounts come from Anne Stevenson.

"Professor Plath"—Rosalie Horn was interviewed by Edward Butscher.

"Robert Lowell's Poetry Class"—Both Butscher and Alexander provide many details about Plath's relationships with Sexton and Lowell.

"Her Poetry"—Butscher's analysis of "The Fifty-Ninth Bear" is included in the addendum.

"Poetry First"—*Sylvia Plath: Method and Madness* and *Rough Magic* examine the reception of Ted's work.

"The Birth of Frieda Rebecca" and "Baby Girl"—Alexander describes the birth of Sylvia and Ted's daughter and the practices of English childbirth at the time.

"Mr. and Mrs. Ted Hughes"—A. Alvarez's first encounter with Sylvia Plath is described in *Sylvia Plath: Method and Madness*.

"BBC"—Stevenson and Alexander describe the relationship between Ted and Lucas Meyers and Sylvia and Lucas Meyers. Details about *Two of a Kind* are also included in the biographies.

"Woman of the House"—Sylvia Crawford was interviewed by Edward Butscher.

"Routine"—Much of Aurelia's feelings about Sylvia's life are included in her introduction to *Letters Home*.

"Elm"—Ruth Fainlight was interviewed by both Stevenson and Butscher.

"Sylvia"—The depiction of the relationship between Ted and Assia Wevill comes from *Rough Magic*.

"A Letter to the Successful Poet"—Paul Alexander includes in his biography that Ted championed the work of Keith Douglas.

"New Affiliates"—Sylvia's beekeeping is chronicled in her journals and letters.

"Shopping in Exeter"—This incident comes from Paul Alexander's biography.

"Can a Vacation in Ireland Rescue Their Marriage?"—Richard Murphy's role in Sylvia and Ted's life is included in *Rough Magic*.

"All the Bitter Things"—*Bitter Fame* explains the origins of Victoria Lucas.

Susan O'Neill Roe and Elizabeth Compton are Devon friends of Sylvia's who are included in every biography. Accounts of their experiences with Sylvia come primarily from Paul Alexander's descriptions, but include details from other sources.

"Divorce"—Susan Macedo's account is from Paul Alexander's *Rough Magic*.

"Finally, a New Home"—Details about the London flat come from Paul Alexander.

"At the Zoo"—This visit to the zoo comes from Alexander. Sylvia's feelings about divorce are expressed in a letter to her mother. Details about the precise terms of Ted and Sylvia's separation are described by Butscher.

"Inconsiderate," "Victoria Lucas," "Saturday Night," and "Sunday Night, Monday Morning"—Trevor Thomas's accounts and background come from Paul Alexander.

"Apparition at Window"—Valerie St. Johnson's memories of Sylvia are chronicled in *Rough Magic*.

"Dysfunction" and "Taxi Driver"—Jillian Becker and her husband's experiences of Sylvia's last days come directly from her book *Giving Up: The Last Days of Sylvia Plath*.

"Saturday Night"—Elizabeth Sigmund conveyed her account of events following Sylvia's death in an article in the *Guardian* dated April 23, 1999.

"Monday Morning"—Paul Alexander includes Myra Norris's descriptions of finding Sylvia's body.

Your Own, Sylvia *Sources and Further Reading*

Aird, Eileen. " 'Poem for a Birthday' to 'Three Women': Development in the Poetry of Sylvia Plath." *Critical Quarterly* 21, no. 4 (1979): 63–72.

———. *Sylvia Plath.* New York: Barnes & Noble Books, 1973.

Alexander, Paul. *Rough Magic: A Biography of Sylvia Plath.* New York: Viking Penguin, 1991.

Alvarez, A. *The Savage God: A Study of Suicide.* New York: Random House, 1972.

Annas, Pamela. "The Self in the World: The Social Context of Sylvia Plath's Late Poems." *Women's Studies* 7, nos. 1–2 (1980): 171–83.

Becker, Jillian. *Giving Up: The Last Days of Sylvia Plath.* New York: St. Martin's Press, 2003.

Butscher, Edward. *Sylvia Plath: Method and Madness.* New York: Seabury, 1976.

Drexler, Rosalyn. "Her Poetry, Not Her Death, Is Her Triumph." *The New York Times,* January 13, 1974. www.nytimes.com/books/98/03/01/home/plath-death.html (accessed September 29, 2005).

Feinstein, Elaine. *Ted Hughes: The Life of a Poet.* London: Weidenfeld & Nicolson, 2001.

Hayman, Ronald. *The Death and Life of Sylvia Plath.* New York: Birch Lane Press, 1991.

Holbrook, David. *Sylvia Plath: Poetry and Existence.* London: University of London, 1976.

Hughes, Ted. *Birthday Letters.* New York: Farrar, Straus & Giroux, 1998.

Juhasz, Suzanne. *Naked and Fiery Forms: Modern American Poetry by Women, A New Tradition.* New York: Harper & Row, 1976.

Locke, Richard. "The Last Word: Beside the Bell Jar." *The New York Times,* June 20, 1971. www.nytimes.com/books/98/03/01/home/plath-last.html (accessed September 29, 2005).

Lyall, Sarah. "Ted Hughes at Last Recounts Life with Sylvia Plath." *The New York Times,* January 19, 1998. www.nytimes.com/library/books/011998plath-hughes-memoir.html (accessed September 9, 2005).

Maroda, Karen. "Sylvia and Ruth." Salon.com, November 29, 2004. http://dir.salon.com/books/feature/2004/11/29/plath_therapist/print.html (accessed March 15, 2005).

Moses, Kate. "The Real Sylvia Plath." Salon.com, May 30, 2000. http://dir.salon.com/books/feature/2000/05/30/plath1/index.html (accessed May 19, 2005).

———. *Wintering: A Novel of Sylvia Plath.* New York: St. Martin's Press, 2003.

Newman, Charles, ed. *The Art of Sylvia Plath: A Symposium.* Bloomington: Indiana University Press, 1975.

Plath, Sylvia. *Ariel.* New York: Harper & Row, 1966.

———. *The Bed Book.* New York: Harper & Row, 1976.

———. *The Bell Jar.* New York: Harper & Row, 1971.

———. *The Collected Poems.* Edited by Ted Hughes. New York: Harper & Row, 1981.

———. *The Colossus and Other Poems.* New York: Knopf, 1962.

———. *Crossing the Water: Transitional Poems.* New York: Harper & Row, 1971.

———. *Johnny Panic and the Bible of Dreams: Short Stories, Prose, and Diary Excerpts.* New York: Harper & Row, 1979.

———. *The Journals of Sylvia Plath.* Edited by Frances McCullough and Ted Hughes. New York: Ballantine Books, 1982.

———. *Letters Home: Correspondence, 1950–1963.* Edited by Aurelia Schober Plath. New York: Harper & Row, 1975.

———. *Poems.* Everyman's Library Pocket Poets. Edited by Diane Wood Middlebrook. New York: Knopf, 1998.

———. *The Unabridged Journals of Sylvia Plath.* Edited by Karen V. Kukil. New York: Anchor Books, 2000.

———. *Winter Trees.* London: Faber and Faber, 1971.

Robertson, Nan. "To Sylvia Plath's Mother, New Play Contains 'Words of Love.' " *The New York Times,* October 9, 1979. www.nytimes.com/books/98/03/01/home/plath-mother.html (accessed September 9, 2005).

Rosenblatt, Jon. *Sylvia Plath: The Poetry of Initiation.* Chapel Hill: University of North Carolina Press, 1979.

Sigmund, Elizabeth. "I realized Sylvia knew about Assia's pregnancy . . ." *The Guardian,* April 23, 1999. www.guardian.co.uk/g2/story/ 0,,297475,00.html (accessed November 7, 2006).

Stevenson, Anne. *Bitter Fame: A Life of Sylvia Plath.* Boston: Houghton Mifflin, 1989.

Sylvia. Film. Directed by Christine Jeffs. Universal Studios, 2003.

Wagner-Martin, Linda. *Sylvia Plath: A Biography.* New York: St. Martin's Press, 1987.

Picture Credits

"Sylvia and her Smith College roommate, Marcia Brown, 1951," courtesy of the Mortimer Rare Book Room, Smith College, © Marcia B. Stern.

"Sylvia and Joan Cantor on the beach in Cape Cod, 1952," courtesy of the Mortimer Rare Book Room, Smith College.

"Sylvia at a Smith College dance, 1954," courtesy of the Smith College Archives, © D. I. Crossley.

"Sylvia and Ted in Boston, 1958," courtesy of the Mortimer Rare Book Room, Smith College, © Black Star Publishing.